Navigator of the Flood

By the same author,
translated into English
and published by The Marlboro Press:

THE WORK OF BETRAYAL

Mario Brelich

Navigator of the Flood

Translated from Italian and with a
Preface by John Shepley

The Marlboro Press
Marlboro, Vermont

First English language edition.

Translation copyright © 1991 by John Shepley. All rights reserved. No part of this book may be reproduced in any form without permission in writing from the publisher, except by a reviewer who may quote brief passages in a review to be printed in a magazine or newspaper.

Originally published in Italian under the title
IL NAVIGATORE DEL DILUVIO
Copyright © 1979 Adelphi Edizioni S.P.A. Milan

The publication of the present volume has been made possible by a grant from the National Endowment for the Arts.

Manufactured in the United States of America

Library of Congress Catalog Card Number 91-61535

Cloth: ISBN 0-910395-79-9
Paper: ISBN 0-910395-80-2

THE MARLBORO PRESS

TMP

MARLBORO, VERMONT

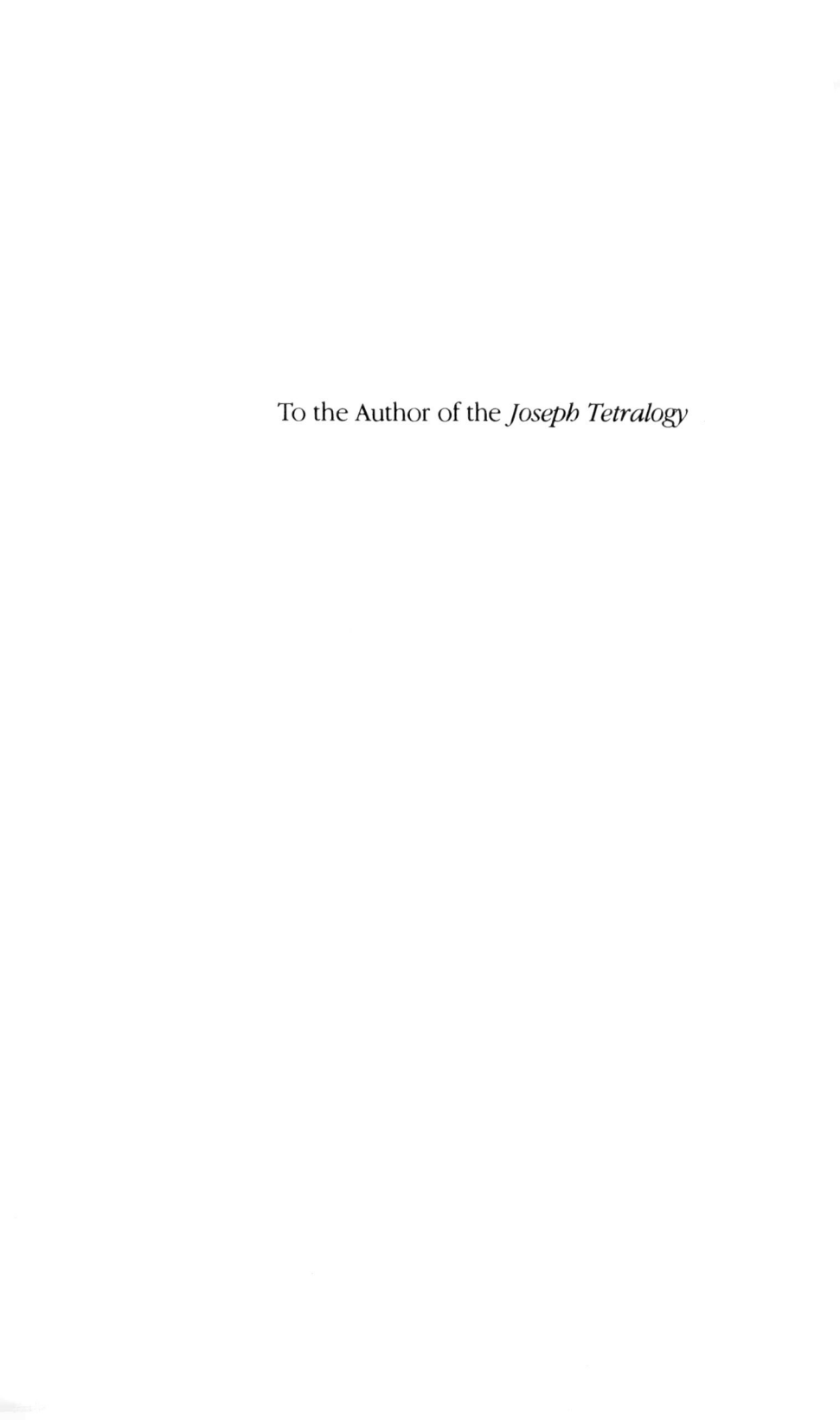

To the Author of the *Joseph Tetralogy*

Contents

Translator's Foreword   xi
Navigator of the Flood
  Prologue   xvii
    I. The deficiencies of omniscience   1
    II. Patriarch without progeny   17
    III. Dissimulation   33
    IV. The altar of the Covenant   61
    V. The fated encounter   81
  Epilogue   101

Navigator of the Flood

Translator's Foreword

> . . . exalted by thoughts of recurrence,
> duplication and the past made present.
> —Thomas Mann, *The Tales of Jacob*

For all the respect implied in dedicating his novel to the "Author of the *Joseph Tetralogy*," Mario Brelich's gesture of homage serves another purpose as well, one that he may even have intended: at the outset, almost as an ironic aside, it points up the difference between the two works. The reader soon discovers that *Navigator of the Flood*, despite its biblical "exaltation," is inspired less by thoughts of "recurrence, duplication and the past made present" than by an irreverent but nonetheless moving assessment of human potentiality. It was Mann's achievement to re-create the biblical world on an epic scale, historically, socially, mythologically, a multilayered panorama in which human figures exist almost as avatars, a series of duplications of themselves stretching back into an endless legendary past. Brelich's aim is more modest but no less adventurous—to render an individual but prototypal inner drama. His concern is with first things, not the eternal return.

Mario Brelich was born in Budapest in 1910, of an Italian father and Hungarian mother. (His father was from Fiume—now Rijeka in Yugoslavia—famous as the scene of D'Annunzio's spectacular exploit, when in 1919 he seized the city with a force of irregulars and claimed it for Italy.) Brelich attended the universities of Budapest and Perugia, where he took a degree in Italian literature, and he seems to have spent some years moving back and forth between Hungary and Italy, before settling in Italy for good in 1946. He died in Rome in 1982.

He was a man of many talents: writer and translator (translating Pirandello, among others), sculptor and ceramist, graphic artist and cartoonist, and according to his widow, the singer Magda László, none of these activities hindered the others, he gave them equal importance and pursued them all "with naturalness—never driven by ambition." As a result of his modesty, his writings remained for a long time in his desk drawer, until finally, in 1972, through the intercession of a friend, he won first prize for an unpublished novel, *Il sacro amplesso* (The Holy Embrace), which brought him to the attention of the Italian literary world. *The Work of Betrayal** appeared in 1975, and *Navigator of the Flood* in 1979.

But *Navigator of the Flood*, though the last to be published, was apparently the first to be written—in 1954. Already Brelich had hit on the form and technique that were to be his hallmark: what Karl Kerényi called the *saggio romanzato*, or "novelized essay." One might wonder why this gifted man, in a relatively long life, wrote only three relatively short novels. Though domiciled in the heart of Italy, he clearly belongs to that distinguished company

*Marlboro Press, 1988; tr. Raymond Rosenthal.

of geographically marginal Italian writers, like Italo Svevo and Umberto Saba, who were born in the former Austro-Hungarian empire and continued to inhabit its shadows. Theirs is a literature of muted colors and shades of gray, of irony, detachment, and wistful resignation. They all share an appealing tone of disenchantment.

As I said, Brelich, unlike Mann, does not labor to reconstruct the biblical world; he takes it as a given and goes on from there. This does not mean that he accepts it on faith. In the story of Noah, as we have it in the Bible, there is no necessary connection between the episode of the patriarch's drunkenness and the flood itself. It seems irrelevant or coincidental, tacked on at the end, as though something had been suppressed, or left out through careless editing. But Brelich insists on the unity, as well as the "intuition," of the biblical legend—of all biblical legends. He states his purpose at the very beginning: to find out why Noah got drunk.

Thus the whole drama unfolds under one spotlight on the stage of Noah's soul. Brelich's originality consists in having grasped the enormity of the patriarch's situation. Face to face with a God who behaves more like a capricious demiurge than the just and omnipotent deity of the theologians, he is the appointed instrument of the most horrendous extermination policy imaginable. Furthermore, his inner torment is made to hinge on one breathtakingly simple observation: he must exploit his people's cooperation in building the ark and gathering the animals, all the while concealing the purpose of it all, and then abandon them to the waters of the flood. Is it any wonder that Noah is a profoundly depressed and guilty man? Why did we never think of it?

Indeed, there is a bland fairy-tale quality to our usual mental image of Noah's ark: the obedient animals entering two by two, the smiling patriarch welcoming the returning dove, the rainbow, the promise of life renewed. We have already forgotten about those who were left behind. Brelich does not forget, and he has also taken the trouble to imagine the physical conditions inside the ark: the noise, the stench, the darkness and discomfort. He touches on them only in passing, just enough to create the setting in which Noah works through his "fruitful state of death," emerging on the other side with some scraps of his humanity intact.

Lest this sound unduly grim, the reader can be assured that this is also a very funny book. Brelich takes all the lacunae, inconsistencies, and absurdities of the biblical account and puts them to profitable use. From this stem both the charm and the impact of *Navigator of the Flood*. The mocking style, marked by an ironically compulsive central repetition of certain key words and phrases, and the obvious affection he feels for his central character, all go to make it a *tour de force* and a worthy precursor to Brelich's still untranslated masterpiece, *Il sacro amplesso*.

The novelized essay receives its fullest and most extended treatment in this second book. It too has as its protagonist an obsessed patriarch trying to negotiate with an intractable God. But it is also the story of a marriage. Fanatical and pusillanimous Abraham, who literally adores his wife yet gives her up without a murmur to Pharaoh and later to Abimelech; and Sarah, frigid, narcissistic, the "most beautiful woman in the world"—these are two splendid human portraits and a perfect match for each other. And again there is the obvious point so likely to be overlooked: Sarah, at the age of ninety, with whom it has "ceased to be after the manner of women," would have to resume menstruating if, as ordained by God, she is to conceive Isaac. How this miracle is accomplished, and the "holy embrace" consummated at last, constitutes the beautiful and startling denouement of the book.

For his third novel, *The Work of Betrayal*, Brelich resorts to a device that, because it is so clearly a device, does not, in my opinion, work as well as it might. The subject is Judas's betrayal of Christ, and in order to explore this "Crime of crimes," the author borrows Edgar Allan Poe's detective, Auguste Dupin, and his sidekick, who discuss the case from several angles—or rather

Dupin expounds his interpretation, while the friend, like the good Watson prototype he is, listens and feeds him an occasional line. There is none of the emotional but ironic identification as with the Old Testament protagonists of the other two books, and Brelich, in hedging his story around with this borrowed machinery, seems afraid of burning his fingers. The creative tension between essay and novel, exposition and imagination—their symbiotic unity, if you like—threatens to unravel, and he brings in reinforcements from Poe to shore it up. Paradoxically, of the three books, this is the one most clearly conceived as a dramatic novel, and it is the novelistic element that suffers. Ultimately *The Work of Betrayal* becomes a rather cold if brilliant intellectual exercise, which is another way of saying that although his mind was fully engaged, his heart was perhaps not in it.

This then is a tentative explanation of why Brelich wrote only three novels. I could easily be wrong, he may have had any number of ongoing projects at the time of his death, with appropriate strategies in mind for completing them, but these three are all we have and this is the pattern, or dilemma, that their sequence suggests. On the other hand, with these three novels, he may simply have said everything he wished to say in this form.

Finally, a word to any fundamentalists out there, whether Christian or Jewish, implausible as it is that any of them would be caught dead reading a book by the likes of Mario Brelich. Still it might interest them to know that Brelich is a kind of fundamentalist himself. I mean by this that he takes the biblical story quite literally. He repeatedly cautions us not to neglect or reject any element of it; again and again he insists that all of it is true. Having said this, he neither glosses nor "interprets," but simply puts his finger on the hidden crux of the story and lets it speak through him. That this happens with so much humor and humanity is the mark of his genius.

JOHN SHEPLEY

Prologue

Ever since our first lessons in religion in our childhood we have been accustomed to consider the drunkenness of Noah as simply the occasion for the exemplary punishment of Ham's filial disrespect. But we must also realize that the Bible was not merely intended to impart moral lessons to schoolchildren. If that were the case, it could have found a more decorous pretext for Ham's punishment than the memorable intoxication of our number two ancestor at an undignified moment in his life.

The holy book is first of all history; what it records happened, in one way or another, in one sense or another, and so we must accept the fact that this venerable man, from whom we all descend, really did on a certain occasion lie naked, indecently sprawled in the middle of the tent, in a state of advanced drunkenness. Thus the question properly arises, in all its compelling interest, as to how the hero of the deluge, chosen by God, came to find himself in this singular situation. Why did he get drunk? Albeit with less impropriety than Ham, but with a little more curiosity than Shem and Japheth, we too step forward to take a look at our progenitor . . .

I. The deficiencies of omniscience

When the Lord informed Noah that he meant to destroy humanity, a whole world crumbled in the patriarch's soul. Apart from the atrociousness of the divine intention, it was distressing and almost unbearable to be forced to recognize that until that moment he had considered life and his relations with the Lord in a completely false light, and to resign himself to it.

Certainly this just and upright man was under no illusions that the world in which he had grown up was the best and most beautiful one imaginable. For him, the memory of Eden was still something more than a mere oral tradition. In his soul it was still alive, marvelous and painful, a magical image that in itself conveyed all the bitter and dreamy nostalgia arising amid the sufferings of everyday reality. Still, he would never have come to suppose that the world, weighed down by the divine curse, was repugnant to its Creator to the degree that had now been made manifest.

In his human naiveté, Noah believed that everything went its way in accordance with a system, perhaps not one actually pleasing to God but that had been established by Him, an order that could be defined briefly as that of the curse, and which no one had violated, at least among the descendants of Seth. Cain, to be sure, had added a heinous crime to paternal disobedience, but this had nothing to do with Noah and his family. His line descended from Seth, whom Eve had borne to Adam after the horrible family tragedy, and expressly to replace Abel, not Cain. Seth had thus taken the place of the beloved son, as his representative and successor, and growing up in the shadow of bloody memories and under exceptionally grave conditions, he had been frightened enough not to oppose the new divine order. This fear, which with the passage of time had been sublimated in the form of a fear of God fed by the awareness of sin, had been transmitted to Enos, and by him to Cainan, to arrive finally, from one generation to another, at exalted Enoch, and so on to Noah, who, always within the limits of human possibilities, could rightly consider himself a just and upright man. Meanwhile not even the fact that in Cain's line, in the distant land of Nod, a new murder had taken place, could be imputed to any of Seth's descendants, and so it was hardly distressing, at the most only odd, that the name of the murderer in that instance was Lamech, just like Noah's venerable father. Indeed, except for this matter of namesakes, there was no connection between Lamech son of Methusael and Lamech son of the indestructible old gentleman Methuselah, other than a superficial assonance between the names of their fathers—assonance, not identity.

Seth's God-fearing descendants had borne the burden of the divine punishment, and it would not have occurred to any of them to wax indignant over the fact of having to work the soil by the sweat of their brows and bring forth children in sorrow. Their tacit resignation to the order of the curse seemed to constitute the pledge of peace, and indeed about fifteen hundred years had passed since the day of the expulsion from Eden without any of Seth's descendants doing anything that, in terms of human judgment, might have provoked the wrath of God. And considering the fact that since that moment the Lord had never intervened in any immediate or personal way in the course of the universe, Noah had every reason to believe that human life, burdened by sweat, suffering, and the awareness of sin, was acceptable to the eyes of the Lord.

Finding himself suddenly faced with the wrath of God, Noah, in keeping with his human shortsightedness, at first conceived the suspicion that perhaps this life yoked to the order of the curse was, in spite of it all, more pleasing to man himself than to God. Indeed, hard as it was to bear, this this life of sweat and pain was, if nothing else, sanctified and exalted by the idea that it was such by God's will and that everything that happened was in accordance with His decisions. This not only enabled one to find beauty and pleasure in this accursed life, but in a certain sense actually made it obligatory, so that it was impossible, even if one tried, to remain insensitive to the deceptive lures of happiness. Even apart from the fact that, in an unjustifiable and inexplicable way, life sometimes appeared beautiful and pleasant, the curses themselves involved various pleasures. Though it was true, for instance, that bread had to be earned at the price of sweat, to eat it was ineffably sweet, and it was no less sweet to restore one's strength for work with sleep, by snatching forty winks from time to time in the shade during the exhausting working day. Even the pains of women required special preparation, and whose fault was it if this preparation involved such sweet voluptuousness? So the fruit of the pains of childbirth was in its turn no less pleasant and useful than the fruits of the soil worked by sweat. Sin and punishment merged in a certain way, and ended by contributing to the glorification of the Lord. Everything led one to suppose that God was infinitely merciful.

In his first moment of confusion, the patriarch also remembered, not without a certain feeling of guilt, that not only did life sometimes turn out to be beautiful and pleasant, but basically it was not, in its entirety, as grim and painful as it had been immediately after the expulsion. But not even this was man's fault. The Lord, who for nine generations had not intervened in a personal and immediate way in the fortunes of the universe, had left it up to man himself to carry out the fulfillment of the curse: it had thus become man's task to ensure his own suffering and create all its prerequisites. It was simply the result of having been thus abandoned that Noah, for example, now lived in a comfortable house, used the wool of the sheep to cover himself against the burning sun or the rigors of winter, lighted a fire to cook his food and dispel the darkness, and, quite unlike his remote ancestor who had still used sharpened flints to remove hard clods of soil, employed hoes and spades whose long wooden handles ended in pieces of especially fabricated iron, an invention of Tubal-cain, son of that other Lamech, the murderer. Possibly he was unaware of this last circumstance, as well as of the fact that lyres and organs, with whose sound his people glorified the Lord on the solemn anniversaries of rustic life, had also been invented by a descendant of Cain, namely Jubal, the second son of that same murderer, Lamech. Indeed, it is not to be excluded that everything beautiful, pleasant, and convenient, and constituting the joy of body and soul, had been imported into the abode of the children of Seth from the distant land of Nod. But even had Noah by chance known it in all certainty, would it have worried him? Clothes, house, fire, instruments, means of refreshment for the body and soul, actually served only to ensure the prerequisites of punishment. For if man, driven out of the security of Paradise, were not surrounded by means of protection and provident contrivances, he would find himself so weak, naked, and powerless in the middle of the immense world that he would be unable to stay alive. And staying alive was also the first and most indispensable condition for toiling with sweat and giving birth with sorrow, that is to say, for the punishment, or the will of God.

These thoughts swarmed in the patriarch's mind after he was notified of the divine wrath, although he did not give them any special value, seeing them rather as preliminary sorties on the path to that true and proper explanation from which he felt himself to be infinitely remote. All too soon he succeeded in ruling out these first hypotheses, reflecting that the Lord could hardly be unaware of what the punishment He himself had established necessarily involved, and on the other hand, that He would have had no need to wait fifteen hundred years, while tolerating things He didn't care for.

These doubts naturally upset the peace of mind of the man who hitherto, in his own just estimation as well as that of public opinion, had always walked with God. He was used to taking this figurative expression, which he heard repeated incessantly around him and which somehow unified his whole existence, in an absolutely literal sense. Thinking of himself, or rather seeing himself as an image, he seemed to be walking on a beautiful path, the path of God, and to be led by the hand of the Lord, just as children are led. But at the same time he believed that all the descendants of Seth also more or less walked with God, and that between him and other mortals there was by no means such a difference as to justify his own position as a favorite and the death sentence that would destroy the others. The Lord must have a very deep and impelling reason to exterminate humanity while saving him. Obviously, to walk with God did not yet mean to understand God.

And still Noah, from that moment on—of this we can be certain—made every endeavor to understand God, and he was the first man ever to complete this endeavor. It was to take him a long time—in the fruitful state of death lasting a year and ten days in the ark—to understand finally something of God's intentions and to evaluate the position of man. Between the forced labor of building the ark and his own moral sufferings, he did not have the leisure to think methodically and glimpse the terrible state of things.

At that time only God considered the situation in exact terms. Today, however, thanks precisely to the initial exertions of Noah and to the insatiable thirst for knowledge of the human spirit, which in the last millennia has never ceased to investigate the mysteries of existence, we have at our disposal much broader perspectives and richer experiences concerning the nature of God than any that that just and upright man could have had when, like a child, he walked with Him hand in hand. We now know, for example—and this is a fundamental notion in our search for God—that the divine nature is very different from the human one, making it quite impossible for us to penetrate it completely, which means that our categories of judgment are never sufficient to measure divine actions and intentions. Noah could have had no idea of this, especially in the astonishment of his first emerging doubts. We, however, basing ourselves on this notion (or rather on the impossibility of knowledge implicit in this notion), and on the progress in relations over the millennia between God and man, are not lacking in a few glimmers of light concerning the ideas nourished by God in patriarchal times, however much the universal divine plan still continues to elude us in its essence.

Today we are aware that the flood was merely the repetition on a grand scale of the expulsion from Paradise, and that Noah, on whom the office of second ancestor fell, occupied the position of Adam at a particularly important stage in humanity's march. But the patriarch's uncertain questions—why had nine generations had to elapse between the two great events? what could the Lord have been expecting from time, which held no mysteries for Him? if He had foreseen what was to happen, why had He been content simply to expel Adam from Paradise rather than exterminating all humanity in embryo?—all these questions were as justified as they were (for him at least) insoluble. Compared to us, however, he had the huge privilege of living the events personally, although this advantage included at the same time the disadvantage of lacking the long view and having to operate with experiences and occurrences, while we can make use of concepts. Thus, for example, Noah "knew" nothing about the forbidden tree in the sense that we know something about it, and considered all of original sin as simply a foolish, and in its consequences tragic, act of disobedience by Adam and Eve.

Much as many details still remain vague or mysterious to us, we glimpse in the tragedy of Eden something more serious and of far wider importance than a simple punishment for childish disobedience. The Creation is shrouded in unfathomable secrets, and besides, the question of why God created man and for what He intended him would take us beyond our immediate purposes. It is difficult to form an idea of what man, the image of God, was like before his fall, and what essentially distinguished him from the animals, reptiles, and birds in the sky, all of whom were provided with a living soul and a certain degree of intelligence. Nor should we attribute a superior intelligence to our first progenitors, since they were images, neither more nor less, which is to say closed and perfect forms not intended for further development. This essential difference, of course, would not have been the result of their physical and psychical shape, but of their situation in Eden. Indeed, while the various wild beasts, birds, and crawling creatures (we don't speak of fishes, since they didn't get there) could have fed tranquilly on the fruits of the tree of good and evil, for man this tree was *taboo*. The decisive moment that gave rise to the process of humanization in this being, who only in his superficially outer features was distinguished from the animals, was undoubtedly this prohibition: in his soul and in his intelligence, essentially not dissimilar from those of the animals, a *ferment* began that made him capable of sin. Until that moment, and specifically due to the prohibition, man had actually found himself truly in a position of inferiority among living beings: both because he was subject to a prohibition, and because, as a result, he could not share the common prize of all the other animals, the fruit of omniscience. Thus occurred the paradoxical situation that animals, like God, were omniscient, while man, the apex of creation, created by God in His own image and likeness, found himself in the most crass ignorance, wherein he bore no resemblance to God whatsoever.

But the spiritual ferment caused by the prohibition began to produce a difference between man and beast. The quite singular reciprocal relations among God, man, and animals began to suffer the effect of the revolution that had been initiated in the human soul. Until that moment animals had been omniscient and man ignorant; from that moment on, a further distinction, subtle but significant, must be drawn: animals were omniscient without knowing it, while man was ignorant but conscious of his ignorance. And this situation was pregnant with possible developments. Indeed, if the animal had succeeded in realizing its own omniscience, it would undoubtedly have become a god, or at least a divine being like God—something that instead happened in a single instant to man, when he, in full awareness, tasted omniscience. But the Lord reacted with lightning speed, and by the expulsion put man *hors de combat*. Of course, the Lord would not so easily have eliminated the animal if, by chance, *it* had been the one to gain an awareness of its own omniscience! Man, in reality, was not a particularly frightening adversary, precisely because he was undernourished as regards omniscience. Oddly enough, little attention has been paid to the highly important fact that every animal is "more" omniscient than man, because with the two days of creation and the years that went by until the expulsion, animals had by comparison acquired an inherent advantage, nibbling at will on the fruit of which Adam and Eve had only snatched a mouthful, and only a single time.

The forbidden tree was a plant of marvelous potency: it was

called the tree of the knowledge of good and evil, or the tree of omniscience, and whoever ate of its fruit became the participant in and master of cosmic connections. He divined all the plans and intentions of God, glimpsed the void in existence, surmised in being the becoming, and was simultaneously means and end, absorbing into himself the harmony emanating from the conflicts in the universe. He who partook of this fruit became an integral and organic part of the Whole, to such a degree as no longer to feel himself a part but the whole. If the tree had received its name in our times, it would certainly have been called the tree of universal existence or of fullness of being. By tasting the fruit of the marvelous tree, Adam and Eve played mankind's great card: through this act, man could in time have become God—had God allowed it.

At this point the mysteries that we dare not try to fathom reappear. What was the Lord's original intention with regard to man? What did He want him to become? Did He perhaps suspend His plan for a moment, allowing His creatures to act on their own initiative, like the players in the commedia dell'arte? Or had He perhaps not foreseen what the humanization of man would involve, namely the birth of human consciousness? Is it possible that He had not realized the danger hidden in the possibility that conscious man would become conscious of the totality of existence? What, indeed, did man lack that would keep him from becoming God, an entity or power not inferior to Himself? Nothing but immortality, which seems to have lain right there, a hand's breadth away from omniscience . . .

The Lord's reaction was instantaneous and of a violence that man resorts to only in extremely critical situations, situations that take him by surprise and attack him from the rear, revealing all the unsuspected nature of their threat. The Lord's attitude suggests that He had not foreseen the developments of the situation in Paradise. And reluctant as we are to cast doubt on divine prescience, we cannot withhold our sympathy from Noah, in whose mind a disturbing doubt—futilely crushed by a zealous fear of God and an anguished sense of guilt—about divine omniscience insistently kept sprouting. Nevertheless there was nothing sacrilegious about this doubt, which had, on the contrary, arisen from a praiseworthy effort to find a justification for God's apparent deficiencies by means of the truly deficient and imperfect human mind.

When, especially in the fruitful state of death in his floating prison, Noah reviewed in his mind the apparent gaps in the divine prescience (from the failure in Paradise to the tragedy of the flood), he became even more convinced in his certainty that God was omniscient, and therefore prescient, but he combined this confidence with the reservation that divine omniscience should not be understood in the ordinary sense of human words. In more modern terms, the patriarch would have said: Divine omniscience is too divine to be able to resemble omniscience as understood by humans. Whenever we reason, speak, or write about God, advancing hypotheses about Him, His qualities, attributes, and manifestations, we must always keep in mind that even our most exhaustive abstractions inevitably remain constructions of the human mind, and so our results are immediately false. Even if God is truly omniscient, to say of Him that He is omniscient, is necessarily false, since His omniscience falls within a dimension utterly inaccessible to any human imagination. So it is not to be excluded, indeed it is fairly certain, that the omniscient God does *not* know everything in the sense we mean by omniscience, and knows everything "only" in a divine sense that transcends every human measure to the point that our "everything" may also not form part of His "knowing everything," apart from the fact that even His "knowing" could be of a nature so different as to prove deficient by our concepts.

If we accept the hypothesis just expounded and thereby recognize the different dimension of divine prescience and omniscience, and ultimately use it to explain everything in them that to the human mind looks like deficiency or a blank, while actually it only renders their perfection more complete, we will fully understand why Noah should suppose that the Lord had failed to foresee various things and had endured a number of bitter surprises ever since the Creation.

Having clarified this rather delicate problem, we will now be able, with a light heart and a fortified faith in divine omniscience, to face that other question which from the beginning had not ceased to trouble the patriarch's mind: What was it that the Lord had been able to expect or hope from man after he was driven from Paradise, and which in the end had not happened, thus forcing Him to send down the deluge? Or else: If the Lord had foreseen, even in the human sense, that sooner or later He would have to destroy Adam's descendants, why hadn't He destroyed them earlier; why instead had He done it afterwards, and even afterwards, not completely? The credibility of our answers should of course be measured on the scale of the hypothesis expounded above, while their author should be considered to be Noah himself, who by passing through these very chains of hypotheses, finally arrived at his great revelations during his burial in the ark.

For the moment, the patriarch was acutely tormented by his sense of guilt and fear of God, but nevertheless he was also tempted by plausible solutions, as he sought to reconstruct the Lord's behavior, while assuming there was some humanly inconceivable necessity that prevented God from destroying humanity altogether. Any other explanation could only turn out to be insufficient. To say, for instance, that the spontaneous and violent reaction by which the Lord had driven man from Eden had also been rash would have been a wholly gratuitous supposition and too humanly base. A God reduced to human proportions would, on the contrary, have had immediate recourse, in his sudden and violent fury, to more radical measures. Here instead was the Lord, after storing up his anger for fifteen hundred years and thus not acting on His first impulse, now deciding again, after serious consideration, not to destroy humanity, or rather to spare a seed of it, which basically comes to the same thing. All this suggested that the Lord was prevented, by the inner consistency of His plan, from abolishing man as a species: such an abolition would perhaps have compromised His own fullness and perfection, which instead cannot be compromised. But considering things from another standpoint, it seems inconceivable that the Lord, with unlimited possibilities of action open to Him and knowing His own plan point by point, had not chosen the best way to punish man, or more precisely to render him harmless. So if He preserved the lives of Adam and his descendants, we can be sure that for some reason it was impossible for him to destroy man, but that on the other hand He no longer had any reason to be concerned for man's sake. If nevertheless He had now arrived, after fifteen hundred years, at the decision to exterminate humanity, this fact can only be explained in the same way that Noah explained it to himself, that is, by the deficiencies of that *sui generis* prescience that did not keep the Lord from being exposed from time to time to bitter surprises.

It would be a piece of naiveté on our part, one not even involving the patriarch, to imagine that God had actually needed so much time to examine and understand the evolution of humanity. Our hypothesis about divine omniscience permits the Lord, at His discretion but not to the detriment of His omniscience, to leave Himself in the dark about certain developments, while always succeeding in time in making the reference to a specific event emerge from His universal consciousness, in order to focus all His attention on it. His surprise, precisely because of His singular gaps in awareness, can be bitter, but this does not mean that it cannot be remedied and transformed in such a way as to conform to the grand plan. According to our historical experience, the gaps in divine prescience derive from its very nature: they are thus necessary and do not thereby compromise its completeness and perfection. By the expulsion from Paradise, the

Lord, so to speak, defanged man, and could therefore allow Himself, more for His own convenience than for the good of man, a period of tolerance, during which He would not be obliged to intervene personally and directly in the development of things. Only by keeping in mind all these circumstances, can we, with our frail human minds, risk the question: What could God have been expecting and hoping for from that experimental period?

Man (meaning, in this particular phase of his evolution, Adam and Eve), driven from the place where he might have had his great opportunity, to a low level of awareness and undernourished in matters of omniscience, no longer represented a danger for the Lord, or at least not an immediate one. This certainty in itself entitled Him to a relaxation of prescience and justified the decision to yield to curiosity, it too compatible with prescience, especially if the latter is not devoid of gaps. At that moment the Lord could without any risks grant Himself the luxury of waiting, while observing what it was that man would undertake with his consciousness, acquired through prohibition, with that handful of omniscience that came to him from a mouthful of apple, with that intelligence of his, now different from that of the animals and which he certainly would sorely need in the misery in which he had come to find himself because of the curse. Conditions did not seem such as to favor man excessively in his enterprises. On the contrary, there was a certain probability that he would cultivate the soil with his own sweat in vain, since he would become automatically extinct, with no need to be destroyed, solely at the hands of now hostile nature, in the same way that animal and plant species die off. Indeed, it may be that the grand plan excluded any action directed at extermination, but not automatic extinction, though it would be too cheap and vulgar to attribute such an intention to God.

Instead we think we are closer to the truth in supposing that the Lord was not at all worried about an eventual reawakening of man's titanic tendencies. He could count with almost absolute certainty on the fact of having, by the expulsion and the curses, frightened the human race once and for all, or at least for seven generations; of having made it, by the sense of guilt He had aroused in it, more miserable than a worm despite that single divine instant of its existence; and again, by not having destroyed it immediately, which could be considered a special favor, of obliging it to feel eternal gratitude. The adventure of Eden constituted a decisive moment in the relations between God and man. The incommensurability of God has never manifested itself, either before or after, in a more resounding manner than this occasion, when He, in Paradise, from one moment to the next, reduced the one who had been the apex of creation, His image and the sign of His glory, to a speck of dust.

In His peculiar prescience, which, as we have seen, lay in another dimension and was not incompatible with a certain intermittence, God, almost as though awakened by an alarm clock, cocked an ear when the descendants of Cain arrived at the seventh generation. These reawakenings are, so to speak, the Almighty's great moments. Our metaphor is trivial only for purposes of comprehension. Were we to put it differently and in a way more consistent with reality, we should say rather that in these instances the Lord recalls to His mind one of the eternal contents of His farsighted consciousness. Here this content was the one expressed by the Bible in the words: ". . . the wickedness of man was great in the earth, and. . . every imagination of the thoughts of his heart was only evil continually." To be more precise and translate this sentence into our language, we must circumscribe what now happened by saying that the Lord again felt Himself in danger and that this impression had come to Him with more or less the same intensity as in the remote times of Eden. Just look: man has not become extinct, nor has he turned out the way he should have, he has been exposed to the rigors of nature, condemned to suffer, and struck besides by the trauma of a terrible fear; he has not become, in the vale of tears of his punishment, a being who, trembling with obedience and servile in his humility, sings hosannahs to God, grateful for His goodness and oppressed by His incommensurability. The difference between Cain's descendants and those of Seth was undoubtedly enormous, and the range extending between the best of the former and the worst of the latter had infinite shadings, but every man, without exception, nourished in himself the nostalgia for Eden, each had a highly developed consciousness and intelligence, and the divine knowledge transmitted to Adam by the forbidden fruit was still latent in the soul of each. These three circumstances, taken together, constituted the possibility of a threat. It could be said, of course, that in the descendants of Seth any tendencies to revolt were still held in check by the fear of God and a sense of guilt, but Cain's people had been strengthened in an incredible manner by the Angels, who with the daughters of men had procreated giants; and what was there in theory or practice to prevent these people, who were continuing to develop in every respect, from launching an attack on the cherubim who guarded Paradise, calmly recommencing to feed on the fruit of omniscience, and taking possession of the tree of immortality? For the moment there was no danger. But to God what man was at that particular moment mattered much less than what he would be able to become were He to rely solely on the workings of the curse, without intervening personally and directly with all the catastrophic weight of His incommensurability.

At a certain moment it had seemed enough to reduce the limit of the duration of human life to a mere 120 years. But nothing demonstrates more eloquently the dimensions that the divine mind attributed to the danger than the decision to wipe the human species, and with it all the omniscient animals, from the face of the earth.

As had happened before in Eden, God's position before man now again became critical. But the mysterious links in the inconceivable divine plan once more saved the lives of men, though compromising their position in their relations with the Lord still further. Indeed, while the Lord found a way to let the human race go on living, this means that at the same time He also found a way to render it even more harmless than before.

The Lord's attention settled on Noah. At the great moment when He remembered the plurimillennial contents of His prescient knowledge, at that instant of lucid omniscience, God clearly saw Socrates and the French Revolution, the theory of relativity and the atomic bomb, painless childbirth and dehumanized man. But all this did not bother Him. It was enough for Him to foresee that Noah's descendants could arrive at all this, but *only* at this, and could no longer become God.

And Noah found grace in the eyes of the Lord.

II. Patriarch without progeny

Our laborious if unfruitful effort to understand God's intentions is not born of presumption, but of the need to place the situation of Noah, our second ancestor, against the background of the divine situation and thereby give it its due importance.

From what we have said so far, it is obvious that in those days God and man reasoned in accordance with two completely different orders of ideas. Indeed, while the Lord was entertaining the thought of exterminating the human race, Noah lived with the profound conviction, albeit not without a few critical reservations, that everything on earth was proceeding in order (the order, of course, of the curse!) and therefore to the relative satisfaction of God. Despite this fundamental difference between the divine and human views, the fact still remains that in those days Noah walked with God, not only according to his own private conviction and in the eyes of public opinion but also really and truly, and the Lord held him by the hand like a child. The distinctive feature of their walking together consisted in the very fact that they reasoned according to two completely different orders of ideas; they had divergent opinions on many things and wished to act in contrary ways. But Noah always found justifications for the Lord, and the Lord, in the final analysis, always approved Noah's deviations.

One of the most striking examples of this walking together along different and frequently opposite paths, and which, oddly enough, has not hitherto been sufficiently appreciated, was the obstinacy with which Noah for a long period of time tried to prevent himself from becoming the second progenitor of the human race, thus setting himself against the sacrosanct order of the curse. But what has likewise escaped attention is the sudden prolificacy that replaced his dogged sterility at the very moment when the Lord was about to decide on the liquidation of humanity, one more example of walking together along different paths. But whatever he was doing or thinking, Noah remained dear to the Lord, because he suggested to Him suitable ideas for modifying the original plan when the time came, without ruining it.

According to the testimony of the Bible, Noah at the age of five hundred begat Shem, Ham, and Japheth, certainly not in the sense of begetting them simultaneously, but rather that he begat them one after another, in rapid succession. This fact leads by deduction, but also with persuasive eloquence, to another no less significant one, namely that this second Adam, to whom in his tribe befell the dignity of patriarch and in the history of the human race the role of forefather, had had no children up until the age of five hundred, in other words until the last twilight flickerings of his virility. This circumstance takes on a particular significance when we look carefully at the genealogical tree of his ancestors, that of the previous generations, where the ages of the fathers at the moment of the birth of their sons, heirs to the patriarchy, are always precisely noted. Thus we observe that five of Noah's ancestors became fathers as adolescents, between the ages of sixty-five and ninety, and only his father and grandfather produced scions at a more mature age, 182 and 187 respectively, but still, compared to Noah, at the age of beardless young studs.

We cannot close our eyes to this curious and—as we shall see—decisive fact, which for us is interesting as an important *given*, but in those days appeared primarily as a curious *fact*, over which Methuselah, the indestructible old gentleman, pondered for a long time. The patriarch Lamech, weary of his multiple functions and yearning for a little peace and quiet, spoke frequently of it, and it was even discussed by families in the tribe, who saw in it bad omens for the future. But, more important, this long and increasingly desperate sterility was a painful and ever present problem for Noah himself, who, being worthy of his ancestors, had every intention of producing descendants for his tribe *quantum satis*.

A certain tendency to delay procreation is undeniable in the generations immediately preceding Noah, and already the fact that Lamech called his firstborn by this name (which means bearer of consolation in our work and the toil of our hands on this earth cursed by the Lord) betrays relief in the midst of discouragement and the realization of a joy that had already seemed doubtful. Similarly, Noah also waited, slightly impatient yet always trusting, for 180 to 200 years; but then seeing the decades and centuries pass, he gradually arrived at a singular state of mind, and indeed a singular situation in relation to himself, his tribe, the order of the curse, and the Lord.

Our source passes over in silence the causes and circumstances of Noah's long and increasingly desperate sterility, a fact that anyway should not surprise us, since the Bible has neither purposes nor pragmatic methods. All this does not mean, however, that the curious fact went unnoticed in its time, and above all it does not mean that there had been no cause for it. Nowadays, in the current phase of our knowledge and awareness, it would be naive to look for this cause in Noah's conditions of life, psychophysical structure, or character. Without denying the possibility that these and other circumstances as well may have existed as superficial causes, visible or tangible, we can be quite certain that in a phase so critical and decisive in humanity's march as the deluge truly was, the regrettable situation of the designated progenitor was not only his own personal affair, but a matter of much more general importance and interest, and of a much more profound nature and higher order, which concerned the whole future human race. From such an elevated standpoint, the superficial causes, about which—since our source remains silent—we will be obliged to venture into absolutely gratuitous hypotheses, will seem to us totally devoid of interest. Organic dysfunctions, a barren wife, psychical inhibitions, taints inherited from nine troubled generations, or even a mysterious vow—was one of these the visible or tangible cause that deprived our common ancestor of children until his late old age? Who can say? With our historical erudition, our knowledge of the customs and traditions of very remote times, the most we can do is exclude some of the hypotheses, but even so an endless number of others would remain, since life is indeed rich in novelistic circumstances. Our curiosity would not mind knowing the secondary cause, but as far as the understanding of things is concerned, it is negligible. Besides, whatever novelistic element may necessarily have shrouded the secondary cause, it looks extremely gray and insignificant compared with the dry facts of genealogy!

Long sterility and late paternity are certainly not exceptional phenomena in human life, and cases of this kind occurred with all probability even in the family circle of Noah himself, although they did not weigh as heavily on the life of a common mortal as on that of a patriarchal candidate. We can be quite sure that in a society in which prolificness was not only a natural process and a socio-economic necessity, but moreover a form of punishment and a celebration of God, in the case of a patriarch's firstborn, himself destined to become patriarch, sterility took on extraordinary importance and the threatening character of an evil omen.

While fully recognizing the extraordinary importance of such dogged sterility, we discard all hypotheses that cannot be taken into consideration as causes, and likewise reject all others that might even be such but would have to be upheld exclusively by our imagination, and prefer to state honestly that the visible or tangible cause, superficial in any case, of this curious fact doesn't interest us in the slightest. Today we know almost with certainty that character and psychophysical structure are nothing but pretexts of destiny; life itself and its variegated circumstances only exemplify fate. Our task can only be to retrace the primary cause, the one located in depth; and fortunately for us, the road leading to it does not pass through the personality and sex life—of which we know absolutely nothing—of Noah, patriarch of a small tribe, but through the well-known situation of the future progenitor in times of catastrophe.

Today, having made some progress in the conquest of the auxiliary sciences of omniscience, we are almost certain, or at least we consider it a certainty, that nothing in the life of the individual depends on chance; and if something seems to depend on it, on closer inspection it always turns out that the fortuitous chance pertains strictly and essentially to the individual, who not only endures but creates, almost produces, its conditions, drawing them forth from his inner essence. Most men, for example, die without ever having dislocated their little finger. There are others, on the other hand, who at every moment manage to break now a leg, now an arm, now a shoulder blade, naturally always by chance, by some incomprehensible accident, at the most through carelessness, but never on purpose. Nevertheless, based on the state of our everyday knowledge, it seems highly probable that accidents of this kind are always deliberate; they are unconsciously desired and provoked occasions against which any protest by our conscious mind is useless, because in us, in the depths of our consciousness, or rather in our unconscious, there is something that wills them, and wills them so strongly and steadfastly that no amount of precautions can bar the way to their fulfillment. A fracture, in all probability, is an excuse or a mask for our destiny, a strategic step, an astute move by our demon. We, as beings provided with reason and free will, are by necessity aware of purposes, aspirations, and interests that seem to us closely connected with our personality. We should not, however, be surprised if something in us, a hidden and buried part of our ego, even if we are not aware of it, plans and carries out things that are totally different, even diametrically opposed. We cannot judge which is right: ourselves, or that "something" in us. We grope our way in the labyrinth of doubts, following the flimsy thread of beliefs, hypotheses, and points of view. But the more peremptory our responses, the more they are debatable. Only one thing seems certain: that we cannot shrug our shoulders at anything that happens to us or befalls us; indeed, we must presume that any broken bone or dose of syphilis comes at the right moment, and that everything that happens to us is an aspect of the stance we take before life, the world, and God.

As with a series of broken bones, or chronic poverty, or a continual lack of success in business, so also we must see the inexorability of fate fluttering over a persistent sterility, while at the same time admitting that even this situation is an equally authentic stance before the universal order, like the choice of our profession or the form of our illness. To put it briefly, Noah *did not want* to become a father. It makes absolutely no difference what he had believed or thought about the matter on the surface of his conscious mind: "something" in him was opposed to paternity, and Noah by his sterility was saying no to life, and especially to the continuation of existence, that is to say, to the task to which his name, both by a whim of destiny and the will of God, has remained unequivocally attached.

Is there anyone among our readers who, after so many preliminary considerations, has not guessed the reason why Noah, or else that mysterious and hidden being that existed in him and was infinitely wiser than he, refused to go on with life? Is there anyone among our readers who still hasn't thought of the deluge? Yet no one need raise the objection that while Noah was consciously doing his best to beget descendants and unconsciously opposed to it to the last gasp, he could not have known of the catastrophe that was in the offing. We would be the first to admit that Noah could not have had even a vague inkling of the imminent, albeit remote, deluge. We insist, however, that "something" in him, which had eaten of the forbidden fruit and still remembered the taste of it, namely the mysterious and hidden part of his ego, was all too aware of what was looming for the world.

Nothing should surprise us in Noah's unconscious stance; his case is similar to the migration of birds in view of the imminent, albeit remote, winter, and which anyway is much less astonishing than the mad flight of wild animals from a forest that will later be set on fire by a cigarette butt inadvertently tossed in the bushes. Noah's stance was also an attempt to save the race, a rather original and radical attempt, in that he wanted to spare it destruction by the simple expedient of not producing it in the first place. Noah, or rather the demon in Noah, wanted to secure his children against the flood by making himself incapable of begetting them. And if beyond this we care to keep in mind that Noah should not be seen only as the candidate for patriarch of a small tribe of shepherds and cultivators, but as a new Adam, the number two founder of the human race, someone who at a certain moment in the evolution of the world, namely the phase that includes the deluge, was Man himself, then there is no way we can be surprised if something in him foresaw the future, and if therefore the demon inhabiting the depths of his consciousness set itself in opposition to procreation by making his dogged sterility permanent.

That Noah, notwithstanding this, should become the second

progenitor of the human race would remain absolutely incomprehensible, if one did not take into consideration the special fact that Noah walked with the Lord.

The Lord's great moment, when He remembered one of the everlasting and infinite elements in His prescience, concluding in His mind that the wickedness of men was multiplying on the earth and that therefore the human race ought to be extirpated, can be approximately specified in time: it took place around the five hundredth year in the life of Noah, who precisely at that time was making his last and most strenuous efforts to beget children and thereby become patriarch in place of the tired Lamech. The Lord, in His great moment, remembered it all exactly and was cheered. It occurred to Him that all men would perish in the flood, but the human race would survive, and He remembered, now with lucid clarity, the role of Noah as well and the reason why he had been saddled with the task of saving humanity.

Aside from the fact that he lived his life in fear of God and was full of a sense of guilt, what made Noah appear particularly suitable in God's eyes for the role of forefather was precisely the furious prolificness with which he overcame his own dogged sterility. Nothing could ever have demonstrated with greater clarity to the Lord that man, if made in the likes of Noah, had become harmless. From that moment on, He looked with a paternal benevolence He had not felt in ages on this son of His who, even while tormenting himself, walked with Him and gave Him a satisfaction such as no human being had ever given Him before. There was a sharp difference between this satisfaction and that conceited *amour propre* that had swelled His breast when He had barely finished molding Adam, and also the nostalgic, almost painful melancholy that He had felt at the sight of Enoch's perfection. Noah brought Him a joy hitherto unknown, a particularly voluptuous, slightly ironical joy, and God at that watchful moment in His singular prescience saw clearly what it was that nourished His satisfaction.

Just look—the Lord exulted to Himself—Noah, or rather the humanity descending from him, has forever lost the battle, the moment he repudiated the sterility suggested to him by the omniscience that lived in the depths of his soul! Here was Noah, who so courteously walked with Him, the first man who, in violation of primordial wisdom, had tried to follow reason; and reason, appealing to his fear of God, his sense of guilt, the traditions of the tribe, and the duties of the patriarch, urged him to procreate, just now, when the best thing was actually not to be born! See how the abyss that after the expulsion from Eden opened between omniscience and the reasoning intellect has widened so immeasurably in this just and upright man that no bridge will ever again be able to connect the two sides! Knowledge of the Whole, which still remembered chaos, and through imperceptible veins drew nourishment from the cosmos, a vessel containing all possibilities and all eventualities, from which He Himself had drunk, was now as though sealed for Noah, and for the first time it was as though sealed for man, more soundly and hermetically than for any other living being! This man, the human being, had for the first time stopped his ears before the voice of omniscience that still echoed within him, in order to follow the command of reason given him by the Lord as a curse!

Such a creature need no longer be looked on with apprehension. In His great moment, the Lord recognized the whole importance of this Pyrrhic victory that Noah had attained with fecundity, desired by his intellect, over sterility, desired by his subconscious wisdom. If humanity in its onward march were to follow the direction laid out by Noah and were to carry with it a sense of guilt and the fear of God as its only memory of the Eden adventure, while letting itself be guided in every other respect by its conscious reasoning, in the faith and conviction that this human gift *par excellence* would be enough for its life and salvation, then man could be pleasing to the Lord, could even bring Him a voluptuous, slightly ironic joy. Man could just as well be wicked and a blasphemer, but one thing now was certain: he would never again be able to harm his Creator.

Into the abyss that had widened immeasurably in Noah's soul between conscious reasoning and subconscious wisdom, the dark gray dull impenetrable masses of the deluge were to pour, cancelling all memories, while mud and slime would cover the furnace of omniscience like an unbreakable bell jar! The gaze of anyone looking back would be met by darkness, and reason would cast beams of light only forward! Long live the human race for the greater glory of God, or for His voluptuous joy, long may it live provided it is harmless and like Noah! May his descendants become the bearers of future life, but perish the seed of Cain and perish all those in whose ears the harmonies of omniscience still echo!

Long live man if he's Noah!—thus the Lord exulted to Himself, voluptuously, almost ironically delighting in the patriarch, who was doing his utmost to violate his own sterility.

While the Lord, in His great moment, was recalling His prescience, clearly grasping the state of things in their most minute details, Noah, the patriarchal candidate, was spending his life as it declined into old age in gloomy sadness. We must not lose sight even for a moment of the fact that Noah at this time knew nothing of what his omniscient substratum instead knew very well; thus the dogged sterility, for which his father and grandfather, shaking their heads, and others, giving him quizzical looks, held him constantly, albeit involuntarily, responsible, had for long centuries gnawed and tortured his soul. No memories of Noah's life in his first five hundred years have been handed down to us, and we do not know in what circumstances they were spent, but one thing is beyond doubt: his long and increasingly desperate sterility cast dark shadows on the virile strength of the future progenitor. And though the hints of disapproval and mute questionings had more to do with the problem of the patriarchy, he tended to see in these manifestations an indiscreet curiosity about his marital life. True, his primogeniture and the patriarchal dignity that awaited him had aggravated still further the sadness and embarrassment arising from his generative incapacity: the hope of becoming head of his tribe diminished from year to year, for who has ever seen a patriarch without progeny? But, in his situation, the thought that really terrified him was that of acting, or rather not acting, contrary to the will of God. Actually he could not have imagined that at that time divine omniscience was going through one of its phases of somnolence, and that to the Lord, who in this period of reduced vigilance was toying with the idea of suppressing all humanity, it did not particularly matter if someone, for the brief time remaining, wanted to increase the population or not. Indeed, had he been able to realize consciously what was ripening in the divine mind, he would in all probability have approved of what his unconscious was telling him: whereby, thanks to his reason, he would have appeared to meet the Lord halfway, by not multiplying—he himself, who walked with God—the race of sinners.

Not being aware, however, of what he knew in his subconscious, it seemed to him that this time he was not walking with the Lord and was in disaccord with the order. Indeed, did there exist any more fundamental and therefore less negligible premise than procreation through the order of the curse, which had installed sweaty toil and painful childbirth on earth? When he considered his situation from this angle, his old moral torments were overwhelmed by his sense of guilt and remorse. Here he was, he himself, by the simple fact of his sterility, setting himself in opposition to the order of the curse and sinning against God!

Noah must have suffered from it very much, and no doubt this suffering became a permanent mark of his behavior. In the course of five hundred years and as a result of this absurd situation with no letup in sight, his continual torments and incessant humiliations plunged him into a gloomy sadness, or a still darker melancholy, which was never, however, the same as resignation. Indeed, while beseeching the help of God, he made tireless efforts to adapt himself to the order of the curse, that is, to beget children, and he made equally desperate efforts to find the key to his accursed state. Since God's will seemed to him the least probable explanation, we can suppose that he sought the cause of his sterility in any other circumstance whatsoever, and assuming he recognized this cause in himself, it seemed to him that he must also justify himself to himself, his family, the tribe, and the Lord, a task that only increased his torment. Somehow he had to tolerate this painful sterility, while demonstrating to others that he was succeeding in tolerating the intolerable. But since he in no way succeeded in tolerating it, he was obliged to put up a false front. We have no way of knowing what this mask, which he wore to cover the ulcers on his pain-racked and humiliated soul, may have looked like on a daily basis. We can presume with a certain probability that his inner crises had set their mark on his appearance, the expression on his face as well as his way of behaving: he may have been clumsy and awkward in his gestures, smiling frequently in a strange way, speaking so quickly as to silence everyone else, or even limping and dragging one foot. Or perhaps, on the other hand, he was locked in an impenetrable melancholy and the dignity of his suffering was his armor against the wickedness of the world. We feel entitled to make these suppositions only by the general observation that destiny, that great film director, chooses by preference types who are suited to the roles assigned them, though this is not a rule without exceptions.

Let all this be said to satisfy those who cannot believe in a character's reality unless they can read his physical and psychical features. But if we do not want to yield even by a hair to our imagination, we must limit ourselves to remarking that in five hundred years his dogged sterility must necessarily have left rankling sores in Noah's soul, and their effects would have manifested themselves in all certainty in his external appearance and conduct as well: this man, destined to become a father at an age when no man, either before or after him, could have dreamt of paternity, was haunted in this extraordinary situation by disorientation, doubts, and moral crises.

We have no reason to suppose that his character and psychophysical constitution underwent any radical change by the fact that at a now absolutely desperate phase of his amazing sterility, at a notably advanced age and to the astonishment and exultation of the tribe of Seth, which in the meantime had grown to become a small nation, he begat in quick succession, indeed almost simultaneously, three sons: Shem, Ham, and Japheth. Lamech, who at the birth of his grandsons felt uplifted by an even greater sense of comfort and relief than when he himself had produced Noah, now with a diligence and zeal far exceeding his age of 680 years, set about the birth ceremonies inherent in his functions as patriarch, from which he could now unfailingly hope to resign. While old Methuselah, who was now approaching the extreme limit of human age, never reached in the memory of man, and who for several centuries had given up keeping track of the demographic increase in his grandchildren, not to mention his great-grandchildren, frequently took pleasure in dandling Noah's firstborn on his trembling knees. Seth's people gave themselves over to celebration, to an uninterrupted celebration of three consecutive years, since they perceived in this sudden and furious fertility of the future patriarch, hitherto irritatingly sterile, the sign of divine benevolence, and looked forward to an unusual increase in livestock and magnificent grain harvests for the next century.

The only one whose joy was not one hundred percent complete was the new father. We can be quite certain that when his wife whispered sweet words in his ear about an imminent blessed event, this man, so sorely tried by suffering, underwent a new collapse in his soul. Lacking any knowledge of novelistic elements, we are not prepared to define the exact nature of the new crisis, and so do nothing more than call attention to what is absolutely certain.

At the root of this moral crisis was his astonishment over an event that smelled too much of the surprising and miraculous. Whatever may have been the cause of his dogged sterility, it was surely disconcerting and almost unbelievable that now at the age of five hundred, and especially after a diligent but not thereby less vain preparation of 470-480 years, all of a sudden and with the greatest naturalness and simplicity, he should succeed in something in which people generally succeed with naturalness and simplicity, while he, up until that moment, had not succeeded. Probably—and let this be said to satisfy the reader's taste for the novelistic, and not as a certified fact—he was assailed many times by awful doubts in relation to his own fatherhood, even though such doubts were devoid of any foundation and appeared all the more unfounded after his sudden procreative furor. But all this aside, one could not pass easily over an event—blessed as it might be—which, during five hundred years of longing, stubbornly persisted in not being realized and now instead had become reality with the greatest naturalness and simplicity. Indeed, when a natural occurrence does not take place, we are left astonished, and when it makes us wait a long time, we wait in astonishment until the waiting itself becomes natural. This waiting then becomes so much a part of ourselves that when the natural thing finally occurs, it looks miraculous and upsets our equilibrium, hitherto assured precisely by our state of waiting.

Noah surely suffered the perturbing effect of this kind of miracle: an effect that, by being repeated twice more, increased instead of diminishing. The vulgar reasoning that was shouted in his ears from all sides, namely that the Lord, in His infinite goodness, had answered his fervid prayers and those of the tribe, did not convince him at all. In his mind, hardened in tortured meditation, loomed the question: Why had the Lord, if He had really had anything to do with this business of blessed events, answered his prayers only now and not before? The anguish that had hitherto tortured him because of his dogged sterility and which—as we know—was nothing but the presentiment of the flood, now wrung his heart with redoubled strength because of his sudden and furious fecundity. Up until now he had mingled his anguish with a sense of guilt for not having fulfilled the order of the curse. But now that he himself had joined the ranks of those who conscientiously followed that order, his increased anguish lost even this weak motive. Something is wrong, he repeated to himself, without being able to say it to anyone else. If I persisted in my sterility for so long and so desperately, he thought many times and not without terror, perhaps it would have been better if the Lord hadn't answered my prayers and had let me die childless!

It was in this form that the inner voice was manifested to Noah, although against his will and accompanied by a sense of fear, since it was completely inexplicable. While he perceived it, he paid it no mind, and having reduced it to silence, he could no longer get rid of it. Naturally he drove away these sacrilegious ideas, and begged forgiveness of the Lord for his unseemly sighs. Certainly he could not yet have known that the Lord, up until that moment, had not interfered in his destiny, and that it had been he himself, Noah, who, by overcoming his own sterility, had suggested a modification in the pre-established divine plan.

Astonishment at the miracle, unmotivated anguish, blasphemous sighs, and the resulting feelings of guilt and remorse not only deprived his paternal joys of purity and serenity, but also increased the confusion in his soul, wounded by so many past conflicts. For us, Noah's sudden and surprising fecundity means simply that he was taking a stance in the face of the cosmic order, no less than before by his dogged sterility, and his anguish interests us only insofar as it arose from his renunciation of a position in which man could still flirt with the divine. This new situation, however, namely the sudden and furious fecundity following a long and desperate sterility, was for the new patriarch, in his daily life as well, the reason for a revolutionary crisis requiring new attitudes, a new face, new modes of behavior; but his adaptation to the new situation was by no means facilitated—as his family naively believed—by a joyous, filial, and grateful abandonment to the goodness of God. If so far his behavior had been odd and his character abounding in anomalies, we can be sure that his newly arrived paternity increased and complicated further the outer manifestations of his disoriented soul. Besides, if we keep in mind that Noah, in the course of five hundred years, had been able to find, in relation to himself and others, a certain justification for his own sterility, and with an immense effort of brain and nerves had constructed a mode of behavior for himself that corresponded to the justification he had given, we can easily imagine how humiliating it was to confess that his behavior had been simply the fruit of overcompensation, and how hard and painful it became for him—and possibly without letting himself realize it—to change his inveterate way of looking at things and make it conform to the new reality.

The one hundred years left to him before the flood were hardly enough!

III. Dissimulation

And then the divine message resounded, causing the collapse of that whole world that Noah, under extreme mental and nervous strain, had constructed in his soul.

The patriarch was already approaching his six hundredth year. Some years before, Lamech had departed the world of the living, and Noah, in exercising the functions inherent in his new position, had likewise resigned himself to dying without obtaining any answer to the problems that were bothering him. Certainly these unsolved problems were secretly consuming him and becoming the source of new anxiety. At his advanced age, indeed, it was no longer only his problems that tormented him, but also the very fact that he was tormented by problems. It never once occurred to him that any of his ancestors might ever have been afflicted by problems or have, perhaps involuntarily and not without fear, pestered Heaven with blasphemous complaints. He therefore, in his fear of God and with his good sense, repeatedly and energetically recalled himself to order, loudly declaring that everything was fine just the way it was, the world was on the right track, and with the disappearance of his own sterility, life had resumed its regular pace in order that the will of God be carried out without further obstacles.

He sometimes thought that if the Lord were suddenly to appear before him and ask him just what it was that was gnawing at his soul, he would be unable to give Him a reasonable answer. It was simply that the secret knowledge that lived in him continued to suggest that something, in spite of it all, was not right. But the patriarch, now supplied with progeny, an essential attribute of his job, and convinced that this offered—in fulfillment of the order of the curse—a new proof that he walked with God, felt somewhat reassured, trusting in the hope that the Lord would never call him to account for those dark thoughts. This hope implicitly and tacitly was based on the observation that, ever since the days of Adam, the Lord had never intervened in a personal and immediate way in the affairs of the world, and it could therefore be assumed that not even this time would He go to the trouble of questioning him.

Contrary to all such reasoning, the unexpected, indeed the unthinkable, happened: the visit occurred, and it was no less terrifying for being the greatest of honors. The Lord came down and spoke to him. True, He did not rebuke him for his nagging questions as to "why now and not before." But He told him great, surprising, astounding things, the amazing and disturbing character of which far exceeded the problem of his dogged sterility and successive fecundity, with the result that Noah, who by this time was cherishing the illusion of a resignedly serene old age, felt as though he had been struck by lightning on the scene of the divine epiphany.

We know that on the surface of the human soul reactions follow one other in swift succession, often indeed intertwining in perfect simultaneity. In a single instant, the same instant, we are able to think of many different things. We are still not fully aware of something and already we've started to evaluate it and reckon its consequences; no sooner are we given an assignment than we're already aiming at its conclusion. In Noah's soul as well reactions darted to and fro, in swift succession or interwoven in their simultaneous presence, while the thundering voice of the Lord resounded like an immensely powerful loudspeaker, and the patriarch's unprepared eardrum was hammered by inexorable observations and bewildering orders. Despite the panic that irresistibly overcame him, the patriarch heard and understood every single word of the divine message, weighed its importance, and vaguely imagined himself engaged in building the ark; there flashed into his mind a scene in which he collected all the animals in the world, while he fleetingly wondered how he would be able to live with wild beasts; but in the same moment he was convinced that when the time came, he would find the solution for all these details, and in the coming and going of these thoughts he felt moved, frightened, humbled, desperate; all this, however, did not keep him from reflecting and telling himself that of course his wife and sons and his sons' wives were the most important, but, alas, how many beloved brothers and relatives he still had! And above all his dear old grandfather, the indestructible Methuselah, was still alive, and what, alas, would become of them? But during, beyond, and apart from all this, he also became vaguely aware of an answer to the question as to "why now and not before," an incredible answer just now, but worthy of further and careful examination . . . Of all these and many other things, Noah thought only incidentally and almost simultaneously, without having the necessary time to coordinate these flashes of thought; but despite this, in his mind and to his eyes, the look of the whole universal order and all of life changed in one fell swoop. It would later require an enormous mental effort and the whole year-and-ten-day period, otherwise inert, of the fruitful state of death in the ark for him to be able to examine everything conscientiously and form an opinion.

For the moment, after the thundering message, he lay there on the ground for a long time, as though struck by lightning, for in cases like this one has to feign death to keep from really dying. This feigned death helped him to avoid any methodical thought or precise evaluation of the importance of these events, and gave him time to clarify in his mind what attitude he would henceforth have to assume. Everything he had heard seemed for now a hallucination so astonishing and superior to any flight of the imagination as to force him to postpone the solution to the new problem as well, namely, how far his experience could be considered real. The most urgent and concrete question, which also preoccupied him during his feigned state of death, was if and what he should tell the others about God's visit or—if by chance the event didn't enter into the sphere of reality—of his vision, hallucination, or call it what you will.

But it was hard to concentrate on this problem too, because the echo of the divine words kept buzzing in his brain like in a beehive. Lying there on the ground, he caught himself trying to sum up briefly the substance of what had happened, or whatever was concrete in this substance. What was concrete was also simple: the Lord would do away with everyone on earth except himself and his family. And then he understood that—at least for the time being—he could not say a word to anyone. Unless . . . unless the whole village was not already informed as well. Indeed, the divine epiphany had taken place on such a colossal scale, with the mobilization of such an apparatus of light and sound effects, as to be seen—provided it was a real happening and not a vision—all the way to the end of the village. But on his way home, seeing that people were going on with their normal lives with the glad and trusting serenity of the order of the curse on their faces, he realized that there was nothing to fear. The message was so strictly personal and confidential in nature that the Lord had obviously taken every precaution to keep anything from leaking out. This being the case, it was no less obvious that he too mustn't say a word about it, since that would mean divulging, and for all he knew also compromising, the divine plan. Anyone else, indeed, might get the idea of building an ark in anticipation of the deluge!

Walking ever so slowly home, he all of a sudden remembered the Lord's mysterious words: ". . . with thee will I establish my covenant." And he felt that this was something extraordinarily grand, whose importance could not be understood at the moment. So far, however, it was clear that in the universal destruction he and his family, seven persons besides himself, would enjoy special treatment, and besides being deeply moving and an honor, this fact was above all, at least at first sight, also extremely useful and agreeable.

On the other hand, this privilege had another aspect so terrible as to overwhelm any human resistance: the other side of the coin was the death sentence for everybody else. Noah was immediately reminded of this when on reaching his door, he met a young mother with her child on her back and she greeted him with the broad courteous smile customary in the relations between insignificant members of the large tribe and its patriarch. Noah usually made no effort to return these smiles. But at that particular moment, his deeply wrinkled face contracted in such a ghastly smirk that the young woman chose to quicken her pace, while covering her child's eyes with her hand.

"She's doomed too, and so is her little one," the patriarch said to himself. "They're sentenced to death . . ." And he raised his hand, veined by work and old age, to his eyes. Then as he gazed over the teeming village, he felt that he was going out of his mind. They too were sentenced to death! All of them, all his people! And all the peoples thronging the surface of the earth, over there beyond the mountain chain, every single human being! In a few days, a few weeks . . . and here his thoughts began to beat their wings like frightened birds. Yes, but when was it actually supposed to happen? Could he have possibly forgotten? Or hadn't the Lord told him? Only at that moment did he realize that he didn't remember, or didn't know, when destruction would strike the earth . . .

We have no right to reconstruct our progenitor's painful and tormenting days in such novelistic fashion. But we are well aware of his problems, of which now one, now another, took precedence, and often all of them came together to torture him day and night, even in his sleep, adding new and darker colors to the sadness that had always been the prevailing note in his mind, at least ever since the first symptoms of his sterility.

Take, for example, the horrible secret shared only by the Lord and himself, and the still more horrible dissimulation by which he was supposed to conceal this secret. There were times when he felt himself on the point of convoking the tribe, standing in the main square and shouting in a loud voice, with all of a visionary's powers of expression: "Run, you people, run for your lives, God is plotting against you!" But it was not hard to dissuade himself from so desperate a gesture. The Lord had countless means at His disposal for getting rid of humanity. Were he to betray Him—what else would he achieve but his own destruction and that of his family? Furthermore, in having to brand an instinctive love for his people with the name of betrayal, he felt his rebellion yield to a stronger wave of fear and a sense of guilt. Everything was the way the Lord wanted it, he tried to persuade himself. But to tell the truth, he could not understand why God should feel such violent disgust with regard to humanity. To his shortsighted human mind it seemed—despite the fact that there were wicked men, perhaps even many, among the descendants of Cain, but of whom, because of the great geographical distance and from having scrupulously avoided all contact, he knew very little—that men, on the whole, were also quite fearful of God and conscious of their guilt, and lived in accordance with the order of the curse.

When he observed individuals, he felt with a certain uneasiness that he was not much better than they, or perhaps not at all, and he found himself unquestionably more guilty than the hundreds and hundreds of children who played around the tents. Hard as he tried, he was unable to guess what criterion might, for the human mind, justify such divine disgust, and to make such a criterion his own. No, this was humanly inconceivable, and a patriarch's heart was certainly incapable of sharing the judgment of the Lord. In this connection, he tried to re-evoke the precise words of the divine message: "The earth is filled with violence through them . . ." We should not be surprised if he, in his human shortsightedness, was unable to understand this remark.

How nice it would have been to be able to go on talking with the Lord, to ask Him a few questions, make a few requests, discuss matters with Him, enter into negotiations, and at least convince Him of the innocence of some! Except that the Lord had spoken or, to be more exact, thundered His observations and irrevocable decisions, only to disappear immediately afterwards among the clouds, in the same sudden and unexpected way in which He had appeared; and He had not even bothered to specify the moment for the deluge. But in the beginning this uncertainty was what least disturbed Noah's soul. Much more important was the fact that sooner or later the deluge would take place and all the people around him—and not just around him, but also beyond the mountains and perhaps within a radius of completely unknown distances—all had been sentenced to death. *When* this sentence—that they knew nothing about and which was known only to him—would be carried out was a question of secondary importance. What was wicked and intolerable was that he, the privileged one, should contemplate the lives of those who, fearful and contrite, but above all unsuspecting, had secretly been sentenced to death, and moreover, that he should constantly have in mind the thing that was hanging over their heads, without being able to reveal what he knew. Worse still: after the divine message, and as a result of it, he must even pretend not to know anything special. But when someone who nobody supposes to know something special and mysterious begins to pretend that he doesn't know anything special and mysterious, the suspicion quickly arises that he does know something, indeed something special and mysterious. This inevitable psychological process did not unfold in the patriarch without visible signs, nor escape the observation of his large family without arousing suspicions. That first ghastly smirk with which, returning from the site of the epiphany, he had greeted the courteous and open smile of the young mother acquired a particular significance in the light of his later behavior, and was considered a first symptom. Indeed, people in the large tribe, which had been vegetating and living without suspicions, began to express the opinion, at first privately and in subdued voices, but later openly, that the patriarch was taking leave of his senses.

Nor was it long before it also seemed this way to his immediate family: the privileged ones. Noah, whose morale in recent days had visibly and precipitously declined, began to make some rather strange inquiries. For instance, he once asked at the table what his sons—all three of whom at that time were already about a hundred years old and thus no longer quite to be considered as children—would think if they were to start building a large ark. At first, they thought they had misunderstood their father's words. Next they pretended to have misunderstood them. Only when the question was repeated for the third time did they summon the courage to ask him what the devil he was going to do with an ark in the middle of a plain, where there was no nearby lake and even the widest river wasn't much use for anything but a place for ducks to paddle. The old man didn't answer, only muttered a few "ahems," but a few days later he brought the subject up again, this time asking how much wood, approximately, and how many hours of work it would take to build a really big ark, one that might even be seaworthy—let's say, three hundred cubits long, fifty wide, thirty high. The hundred-year-old striplings snickered to themselves, and one of them asked calmly whether his venerable father perhaps intended to go whaling. Another observed more politely that so far nothing had come of his father's ambitions to be a navigator. The third offered the suggestion that if this idea was really so important to the old man, they send someone to the seaport, on the gulf that lay several days' journey away, where there would certainly be experts and workmen specializing in naval constructions. Again the patriarch confined himself to a little muted grumbling. It was, of course, very difficult to justify the unjustifiable or to invent some complicated story in place of the simple truth. Noah had always been a simple and truthful man. Even when it had been a matter of justifying his own dogged sterility, he had always spoken in perfectly good faith, nor had he ever found himself in a situation in which he was obliged to lie: all his just and God-fearing life, his position and dignity had excluded the possibility of falsehood. As a result, his total incapacity in this area was now apparent. He was unable to invent a plausible story.

For our part, we rush to the defense of something that is not only worthy of esteem but should require no defense: we defend the inability to lie demonstrated by Noah. Let us put ourselves in our progenitor's shoes, with the whole secret and all those orders weighing down on him: who can say that among us there would be a single person so clever and subtle as to be able to offer plausible reasons why the leader of a tribe of shepherds and farmers, living in the middle of a plain, should need a boat for the purpose of plowing the high seas? Noah merely confined himself to mumbling a few unintelligible words, and since he was not capable of lying but only of keeping silent, heroically resigned himself to the fact that everyone, whether secretly sentenced to death or secretly saved, was forming an unflattering idea of his mental state. Having later considered the urgency, importance, and difficulty of his task, a task also to be carried out in secret, he was to confirm that unflattering idea with ever new, surprising, but indispensable words and acts.

That there was a screw loose in the brain of the paterfamilias and tribal chief was also shown by the anxious interest he suddenly began to take in the health of his grandfather Methuselah. From the confused and uneasy questions, repeated with extraordinary insistence, about the state of the indestructible old gentleman's health, the patriarch's wife, sons, and daughters-in-law got the impression that Noah, for all his fond concern, would have liked to hasten his grandfather's death.

Apart from the fact that in wishing for and expecting the death of progenitors there was a touch of sacrilege that dismayed everyone's moral sense, especially since this particular progenitor had greatly exceeded the limits of human life and had thus become not only a symbol of the absurd hope for earthly immortality but also an object of pity in the eyes of the whole tribe, Noah's behavior was incomprehensible for another reason as well: that he not only shared a hundredfold his people's compassionate feelings for Methuselah, but could not have had even the slightest motive for desiring the indestructible old man's death. How could he feel vexed by that old gentleman, who for decades had spent his days dozing and whose presence cost him no worry or effort? Methuselah by now asked nothing of anyone, nor was he even able to tell one person from another among those who came to see him, paused on the threshold of his room, and rested their piteous gaze on this living mummy. Beyond the obligation to feel pity, willingly accepted by all, the old man was no burden to Noah whatsoever.

But now the patriarch went to see his grandfather more often than ever. He was capable of spending whole hours at his bedside, anxiously observing every least sign of life: often he leaned over the old man's face, as though waiting to catch the last breath, the last heartbeat. Rumors about his curious behavior spread far beyond the walls of his home, and people's astonishment exceeded even the compassionate shudders aroused by the patriarch's madness.

Noah himself could no longer tell exactly where his methodical insanity ended and his actual madness began, for while he consciously assumed the role of madman in the interests of the divine plan, a secret shared only with God, still the inhuman grandeur of his important, urgent, and complex task, and the emotions inherent in it, brought on some truly serious crises in his soul, already wounded by its moral conflicts. Yes, even the question of his grandfather was one that contributed to his sufferings to no small degree. To put it bluntly, did God not care to make room in the ark for the indestructible old gentleman, or had He simply forgotten to say? Was it conceivable and defensible to leave Methuselah, that increasingly unsuspecting old creature, on his deathbed, abandoning him to the waves of the flood, while having at the same time meticulously to reserve space in the ark for two hyenas and two camels, in accordance with their species? Oh, what wouldn't he give to see his grandfather expire before the heavens opened their sluices!

One hope, in this sense, was truly present: come to think of it, it may have been there for centuries, just as for centuries there might have been the fear that in spite of everything death would finally gain the upper hand over the indestructible old man. Like the fear before, so now the hope was justified that after 969 years, his grandfather Methuselah would simply sink into eternal slumber, rather than having to drown miserably like the unwanted kittens that get thrown in the river. Noah silently praised the Lord, though not without reservations, for not having given him instructions about what pretext to use in starting to build the ark. The perplexity caused by this situation somehow granted him a little time, even against the Lord, to hope for Methuselah's natural death. And it also gave others time to die a natural death, without having to perish by the hand of God.

The patriarch's moral confusion was increased by the fact that the Lord had left him in the dark about the date of the cataclysm. What would happen in the end if the flood should begin at a certain moment and there was still no sign of the ark? But Noah nourished hopes even in this regard. The Lord obviously could not fail to take into account that even working at a heightened pace, the construction of such an enormous ark would take time; and in taking this fact into account, He would not neglect the need to prepare public opinion, the need to prepare a naive population of shepherds and farmers for this unprecedented undertaking. The fundamental trouble was simply that Noah, a just and upright man, had not the faintest idea of how to make the execution of the divine command plausible while it still had to be kept secret. And yet he was certain that the Lord's patience could not last indefinitely.

If in the Lord's presence he had had to preserve all his calm and strength of will, in the presence of men he had no way out but madness. It was an oddly complicated psychical process, this madness of Noah's. For while he preserved all his lucidity with respect to his task, the equilibrium of his mind was at the same time truly shaken, and on the other hand this real mental breakdown also served him as a pretext in being able to carry out the divine command. Indeed, who would have been able to assign peaceful shepherds and farmers the astounding task of going into the woods and mountains and capturing every species of animal, not one but two specimens, one of each sex, from lions to snakes, giraffes to porcupines, and bringing them carefully and unharmed back to the village? And above all, who would have been able to give the order to employ all available manpower in the construction of a gigantic ark in the middle of the immense plain, where even the widest river was useless for anything except ducks? Who would have been able to give such mind-boggling orders without the slightest explanation? Obviously only a madman.

The patriarch was mad! This unequivocal observation was by now common knowledge and the source of indescribable depression in the tribe. To be sure, the figures of the patriarchs were surrounded by legends, and each one's name was linked to some great action or idea that filled ordinary people with wonder. But even if the greatness of the elect was for ordinary people cause for wonder, such wonder was always combined with a sense of veneration as well as a touch of vanity that made them think: see, the great man had done things that even we ordinary people approve of and would have done ourselves, had we been great men. But Noah's actions aroused nothing but talk and sadness. Oh, it would never have crossed anyone's mind to build an ark in the middle of the plain, in the valley surrounded by high mountains, and no one would ever have thought that the tribe of Seth had need of a zoo. Noah too might be a great man, but when greatness transcends the limits of the human, you can no longer distinguish it from madness. And this was unquestionably madness.

There was not a single person of mature mind in the God-fearing tribe who took the matter lightly. The patriarch's madness was considered a bad and threatening omen, just as a hundred years earlier his sudden fertility had seemed to portend an imminent era of peace and happiness. Now people had no choice but to serve and second the patriarch's madness, while praying for him to the Lord. For there was no one on earth to turn to for advice. Kindly, tired Lamech had left the world of the living some years before; Methuselah, the arch-patriarch, was already too old and was spending his last decades with one foot in the grave. Shem, on the other hand, the hereditary patriarch, though a calm, serious, and God-fearing young man, counted with his mere hundred years as a snot-nose, and there was no point in asking him for a decision or even a suggestion. And so the members of the tribe were reduced to discussing among themselves the way things were going, without reaching any conclusion because really nothing could be done about it. Tacitly they decided to give up any serious search for a new solution, at least until the patriarch's madness took a dangerous turn, and resigned themselves to satisfying his mad but harmless whims.

Although Noah's instructions were exceptionally trying for the tribe, they were also a source of entertainment, especially for the young. Furthermore, they brought a little novelty and variety to the monotony of work in the fields and pastures: setting traps on the woody slopes, preparing nets and snares for birds, collecting every kind of worm and insect, to bring them triumphantly in the evening to the patriarch, who, with the assistance of others chosen for this task, examined the wholeness and sex of the most repugnant earthworm and added it to the other specimens in the collection. The zoo grew steadily in size, and women and children spent hours and hours in front of the cages, admiring the rare animals that otherwise they would not have been able to see except in the middle of the woods or on the mountaintops.

At the same time, work had begun on the construction of the ark. The patriarch himself directed operations; he was everywhere at once, personally supervising the daily transportation of gopher wood, and assigning the most skilled workmen to carry out the plans he himself had designed, explaining to them that the ark was to be on three levels, with the door here and the window over there. He took an interest in the slightest details, joined in all discussions, and even in problems of pure engineering demonstrated such keen understanding as to confirm once more the common opinion about his state of madness.

The more the work progressed, the more the patriarch suffered. He was increasingly oppressed by the tragic nature of the situation, and there were times when, feeling he couldn't stand it anymore, he was obliged to take refuge behind the screen of madness even in the presence of the Lord. By now it mattered nothing to him that he was treated like a madman, that now and then he caught a smile of commiseration or a disrespectful sneer, nor did it bother him when others stood in front of him, their knees trembling in sacred terror, or watched him depart with visible relief. Little by little even his grief for old Methuselah lost its importance. The sainted old man, moribund for a century, seemed to have dug in his heels at the edge of the grave.

Noah did not even suffer too much at finding himself treated in his own home like an unwelcome dog: his wife no longer dared to share the bedroom with him, and even the solemn patriarchal meals were no more, since with the excuse of work, the family sometimes ate before he did, sometimes after, while he himself often had to be content with a frugal snack consumed on the work site. Since it was logical, none of this offended him, and he could also console himself with the thought that soon, unfortunately, the hour destined to justify him in the eyes of his privileged family would strike. But what about those who had been sentenced to death? He thought with terror of the hour when his behavior would likewise be clear to the eyes of the doomed! No, this was an idea to which it was impossible to become accustomed, and no one in his right mind could resign himself to it: he felt the madness winding along the convolutions of his brain, and almost wished and hoped that at a certain moment everything would grow dark in and around him. No, there was no satisfaction in seeing the execution of the divine command proceeding so smoothly; on the contrary, every single cubit added to the width or height of the ark also added something to his sufferings. It was indeed excruciating day after day to see these young men working, heedless and amused, and whose high spirits froze only on his appearance. And, in general, it was enough to drive one crazy to have to make unsuspecting people work, so that on some fast-approaching day, he and his privileged family could take possession of what the doomed had built, and then abandon them to their horrible fate.

The day came when the ark was almost ready. Only a few accessories were missing, the bolts for the cages, the locks for the door, and the roof at the stern end remained to be tarred. Noah, thinking to gain a little more time for Methuselah and his people, decided to paint the ark green. But the vessel of the flood was to remain black . . .

What he had feared and longed for came to pass, though not quite the way he might have wished. In fact, he had dreaded what at the same time he had wished for, and had feared it so much that often he woke up at night with a start, thinking it had already arrived. But the stentorian voice, as though from a loudspeaker, had always turned out to be a hallucination, one form of his frequent nightmares. Might the Lord never appear to him again! Might the terrible honor that had been spared his ancestors never be bestowed on him again! But should the Lord nevertheless appear to him, in that case he would speak up! Yes, he would try to persuade Him to have pity, to get Him to desist from His decision, or to save what there still was to be saved, asking mercy for Methuselah and for some others! Or else asking the greatest mercy of all: to be allowed to share the fate of everyone else!

But one night the roar of the megaphone did not cease when he woke up. The voice, accompanied by a pervasive tremor and a blinding light, pinned him inexorably to the ground, and in vain did he moan, gasp, cry out—from this nightmare he was not allowed to awaken. The Lord spoke and he, stunned, his head throbbing, concentrated all his strength in order to hear.

For it wasn't easy to follow the Lord's words! Because he had awakened so suddenly, his mind remained as though paralyzed, and then as he managed to gather his strength, his thoughts, as though constrained, stayed fixed on one single purpose: to speak up, to speak at all costs, to the Lord. But when finally he was able to follow the Lord's words attentively, the roar of the megaphone ceased, the light went out, and everything around him returned to its normal condition much more suddenly than he would have thought possible. It had been a brief message.

He could remember nothing exactly, everything had to be reconstructed. Numbers and words danced a diabolical reel in his head. Seven days, forty days, two animals, seven animals . . . or seven pairs of animals . . . How was it all about? The actual imminence of the cataclysm was less terrifying to him than this confusion about the number of animals. Had he misunderstood the previous time? Or was he getting confused now? Gradually it dawned on him that seven pairs were not required for all animals and birds, only for the clean ones, but nevertheless a huge and unexpected effort awaited him for the brief time remaining. And—a frightful task that seemed simply impossible to carry out—the whole ark had to be rearranged inside, to adjust it to the increased number of animals, the dimensions of the cages already installed had to be reduced, and a good part of the space reserved for the family's sleeping mats sacrificed. How could all this be done in seven days? There was no time to lose. Forget about painting the ark green! It would be cause for rejoicing if he succeeded in collecting and installing the missing animals and loading the provisions.

After much twisting and turning in bed, with the room once again dark and silent, he regained the certainty—a certainty he could swear to—that it was not he who was mistaken, it had been the Lord who had said two different things, mentioning two animals the other time, and now seven pairs of animals. Was it possible that He had changed His plan in the interval between the two messages? Or was the Lord perhaps wrong? It occurred to Noah, filled as he was with a sense of guilt and the fear of God, that a precision for detail was not the Lord's strong point, or at least He weighed the importance of things differently from the way that might have been expected of Him. Well, never mind. What about the animals, one pair or seven pairs? Noah decided to do whatever was humanly possible in favor of the higher figure. But there was a much more serious problem: the provisioning! With His peculiar priorities, the Lord had dealt meticulously with matters that were totally superfluous, namely, those that could even have been settled by the human mind, while He had left a series of extremely vital and important things in the utmost obscurity. It was Noah's opinion that even he would have been able to calculate the proportions and measurements for building an ark big enough to hold his family and the animals (counting on two of each species): in fact, had it been left up to him, he would have made it twenty-five cubits longer and ten cubits higher, and for greater comfort added a fourth deck, something that would now have proved to be especially useful, since he had to lodge not two but fourteen specimens of so many animal species. But in this respect the Lord had tied his hands, while for the more essential points He had not even given him any useful suggestions. Indeed, what kind of practical suggestion was the command: "And take thou unto thee of all food that is eaten, and thou shalt gather it to thee; and it shall be for food for thee, and for them" (that is, for the animals, but, alas, two of each species!)? Instead of the cubits and the inner arrangement of the ark, it would have been incomparably more useful to know for how much time, how many days, how many weeks, or—God forbid!—how many months those food supplies would have to last. Wouldn't it have been more logical to say immediately, in the first message, that during the deluge it would rain for forty days and forty nights? Even this wouldn't have been all that much, but still it would have provided some frame of reference: at least it would have made it clear that it wasn't a question of days, but of months. Instead the Lord had confined Himself to conveying the information that all persons excluded from the ark would be doomed, but He hadn't given a single thought to protecting from starvation those He wanted to save. If only He had at least said what kind of deluge it would be, how much time they would have to spend in the ark, and what the conditions of life would be like after the cataclysm! How little effort it would have cost Him to specify the kind and quantity of food that needed to be stored!

Next day at dawn the frightened tribe saw that Noah's madness had entered a new phase. He ran back and forth around the ark like a lunatic, and sent messengers to the most distant villages to summon the people. Though not long ago he had promised his workmen a little rest, now he began to dog everyone's heels, and so the first rays of the rising sun fell on people already loaded with heavy sacks or large animal cages. The faces of Shem, Ham, and Japheth, their mother, and their wives flushed with shame and they could barely hold back their tears in receiving the compassionate looks of those who were dripping with sweat under their enormous burdens. How painful and humiliating it was to see their father, this man who had once radiated dignity and majesty, bustling like a madman around the product of his sick mind and imposing such brutal exertion on his faithful people! Their hearts were full of bitterness, and they felt a profound gratitude for the compassion of the others.

Despite Noah's frantic bustling, the work did not proceed at a reassuring pace. His plan for arranging the animals had collapsed as a result of the Lord's new commands, while often what had seemed perfect on paper did not in practice match the reality of things. Who would have thought, for example, that at the last minute they would have to break a hole through the ceiling between two decks for the giraffes, or install narrower bars on some of the cages to prevent the smaller animals from escaping? Where it was possible to place the cages one next to another, it turned out that their inmates could not get along. Also the arrival of the new animals, a few at a time, caused continual inconvenience, and the situation was unduly complicated by Noah's order to double the quantity of provisions already packed and stowed, the new supplies being added in a great hurry and as a result in the most complete and chaotic confusion.

We do not think anyone can accuse us of granting too much freedom to our imagination in recounting the vicissitudes of the construction of the ark. This is how it all must have happened, more or less, and even if we may be mistaken in details, we are absolutely sure as far as the substance is concerned. But now in the course of our story we come to a detail that excites the writer's imagination to an extraordinary degree, and we are imposing an exceptionally strict discipline on our pen. This detail, so exciting for the imagination, is the death of Methuselah.

Our source does not say how and when the indestructible old gentleman died. Only indirectly, and by making indiscreet calculations from the dry facts of Seth's lineage, does it appear that Methuselah passed to the other world in the very year of the deluge, and so it is hard to avoid the horrible suspicion that he too, like all the others, perished miserably in the waves. The uninformed, however, like to think that he may have left the world of the living previously, on an ordinary day.

The Bible's sparing words, or rather its silences, leave open the same possibility to both the horrible suspicion and the prosaic demise, but without offering any sufficient reason for adhering to one or the other hypothesis. When therefore the uninformed and the malicious hasten to accuse us of being arbitrary in supposing that Methuselah was still alive after the second divine message, we point out to them that they have no more reason to doubt it than we have for being certain. But there is really no need to reach a definite conclusion: our purpose is achieved, even making a few concessions to the skeptics, if we limit ourselves to the quite likely, and for us satisfactory, hypothesis that at the moment Noah and his family entered the ark Methuselah was in some way still alive, while in a certain respect he was already dead.

In this hypothesis we are not guided by any wish for paradox, but only by our strict adherence to the chronology of the patriarchal epoch. When you consider that Methuselah lived for almost a millennium, his old age must be reckoned at a few centuries. And if a hundred years before the deluge he had hardly enough strength to show his preference for Noah's firstborn, his most important great-grandson, by trying to dandle him on his knees, it is hard to see how, after this event, more than one or two decades could go by without his entering into a phase of senile feeblemindedness. But the process of enfeeblement could not have been shorter or less impressive than his whole life, which means that the indestructible old gentleman would have spent at least three or four decades on his deathbed, awaiting gently and without suffering his final hour, which in keeping with the particular pace of his life, he knew would be prolonged for several years. At the moment the deluge was announced, we can be sure that the sainted old man was already, so to speak, in his death throes: he had already arrived at his final minute, which at this point could not last more than a few weeks or at most a couple of months. We can therefore feel confident that the moment when Noah went to bid him farewell was likewise the last moment in Methuselah's life, or to put it more precisely, the moment when the ordinary mortal ceases to be alive and becomes a dead person. Noah would have noted with indescribable relief that it was no longer a matter of the final minute, but of the final instant. Though there was no time, given the extreme urgency of the divine command, to close his grandfather's eyelids and accompany his coffin, he entered the ark with the welcome consolation that this final instant could not last more than a few days.

Freed thus from an oppressive worry, he still had no chance to think about mourning, nor about his own relief. Inexorably, the week of the embarkation arrived; the seventh and last day of the last week arrived. During that last week the patriarch took refuge more than ever under the cloak of his madness. He needed to, for now in addition to finding pretexts and excuses in the face of public opinion, he also had to justify himself to his immediate family, those who unbeknown to themselves were the privileged ones. Of course, he took advantage of this last week to drop a few hints in the presence of his wife, sons, and daughters-in-law, allusions to the fact that now sooner or later they would all have to enter the ark. The members of his family, who for months had lived in the stifling atmosphere of the patriarch's madness and had had time to learn to take his most bizarre remarks seriously, were left in a state of terror after the first hint, since they knew very well that even here it was no joke. As a last resort, however, they tried to turn it into one, and much as it might seem to show a lack of respect before such a solemn and venerable madman, they asked, with trembling lips and what they hoped was a light and cheerful smile, such questions as: "So when are we taking a boat ride, father?" Or: "Why should we get on board before it's time to leave?" And Ham, in rather sharp tones: "How the devil do you expect to navigate without water? It wouldn't be a bad idea, father, to give it a little thought." Noah lost his temper and replied: "Since the Lord has given us a boat, He'll surely give us water to go with it!" And this retort had a wonderfully calming effect on his soul. Soon thereafter he peremptorily ordered the family to transport the indispensable furniture and household utensils into the ark, taking everything that might offer some relative comfort on a long voyage.

It needed all the authority of a patriarch and the goading tyranny of a madman to make the terrified family set out in the direction of the ark, which lay, its hulk black with pitch, on a broad meadow adjacent to the village. When the news spread that they had left their home in order to move, bag and baggage, into the ark, all the members of the tribe appeared on the doorsteps of their houses, casting commiserating looks at the three boys and the women. Noah himself, more gloomy and deranged than ever, marched with decisive steps at the head of the group, looking neither left nor right. But the others, with tormented looks, sought sympathy from those standing in their doorways, and motioning toward the ark, kept repeating in low voices: "Have pity on us, good people. *That's* our home from now on!" And as a sign of compassion, people raised their eyes to heaven.

The sun that morning blazed in the pure blue of a serene sky. Noah's family, approaching the ark, could already hear from some distance away the chaotic noises of the largest caravansary in the world, and the looks they exchanged were filled with despair. But they put up no resistance, and followed the patriarch as though they were tied to him by a rope as he stepped resolutely through the doorway of the ark. An oppressive darkness and an indescribable stench struck them like a fist full in the chest. Even the patriarch gave a start. He seemed to have a moment of hesitation—the others thought and hoped he was about to turn on his heel. But no, he proceeded relentlessly along the dark corridor with its row of noisy, stinking cages.

The others followed him as though hypnotized. And at a certain moment they all stiffened, and turned their heads: the great hulk of the ark resounded with a loud, somber clang. The Lord had slammed the door behind them . . .

Let us spare ourselves a description of their thoughts and feelings, and the words the seven of them said to each other before they learned that they were the privileged ones. We leave to the reader's imagination their emotion at the moment when the door, pushed by a mysterious hand, closed behind them, and they realized they were prisoners in a dark and stinking structure echoing the chaotic voices of myriads of animals, and whose misshapen hulk lay uselessly in an abandoned meadow, arousing the amused compassion of those who were left outside.

Having entered the ark, the patriarch retired immediately to a dark cubbyhole, which he had reserved for himself despite the unexpected increase in the number of animals, and his first act was to rend his clothing and scatter ashes on his white hair. Then he sat there motionless, staring into space without a thought in his head. It occurred to him, purely automatically, that he ought to pray, but he had nothing to say to the Lord.

His unhappy family waited a long time before they dared to disturb him. But at the hour of dusk, when the hungry animals set up a diabolical concert of howls and began rattling their cages, they all felt a suffocating anguish growing in their hearts, and rushing to the tiny cubbyhole, threw themselves with loud laments at the patriarch's feet. His wife, beside herself, her voice breaking with sobs and shrill from excitement, threw in his face all the questions, all the accusations, all the sufferings that had ceaselessly tormented each of them for so many months. Her hands clasped, she harshly demanded that he speak up for once! What did all this mean? How did it make sense? Or maybe it was true, what everyone believed, that he'd taken leave of his senses and gone crazy? But if he'd gone crazy, he should do so on his own and not bring ruin on everyone else! That he had no right to do! He must answer, if he still had any respect for God, answer immediately! And her torrent of desperate words mingled with the plaintive chorus of the three younger women and the vigorous protests of the vexed sons. Noah simply gazed at them, with staring eyes, but his hands trembled as he crouched on the floor, his clothing torn and his white head sprinkled with ashes. His silence and immobility, which clearly only served to control a powerful inner emotion, were intensely and fearfully intimidating. But the others were in no mood for further intimidation. Kneeling before him, weeping, shouting threats and curses, shaking their fists, they demanded an answer, while the animals, sensing the collapse of the human world order, indulged in an unrestrained and chaotic orgy of cries, squeals, and howls.

All of a sudden, Noah, as though listening intently, raised his hand slightly and stared at the ceiling. At this gesture, the seven fell silent, and by a miracle, even the animals stopped howling for a prolonged moment. Everybody in the ark cocked an ear. Then the patriarch raised his sad eyes to them and pointed upward.

They heard a muffled, monotonous patter on the roof and sides of the ark.

It sounded like rain . . .

All this lasted for a long moment, but it was a striking scene. All of them understood something, something terrifying, without being able to tell what it was. At the same moment, what their deranged father had said one day not long ago flashed through all their minds: "Since the Lord has given us a boat, He'll surely give us water to go with it." There was something ghostly in the slow patter of the raindrops, amid the silence that seemed miraculously to have descended on them. This ghostly spell only dissolved slowly, gradually, little by little, and thinking about it, they began to suspect that they were the victims of a hoax. Indeed, there was nothing strange in the fact that it was raining, especially at this time, on the eve of the rainy season; it had rained before, many times, and when it did you at most refrained from going outdoors, you certainly didn't move from your comfortable ancestral home into a dark and stinking boat that had been turned into a zoo. For all its ghostly effect, that soft sound of rain actually explained nothing at all, and the old man would have done better not to ask them to believe that a simple shower had made it indispensable to move into the ark. Was he expecting the ship to be set in motion? By this reasoning, they were able to shake off the spell, and their reaction was to get angrier than ever. Again they started shouting in chorus, with shrill voices and curses, while the animals too intensified their infernal uproar.

Then the patriarch told them everything. With no additions or comments, he reported the two divine messages. Of himself, his behavior, his thoughts and state of mind, he said not a word. And this was not out of malice, nor to take a subtle revenge, much less with the pedagogical intention of saddling his family with the grave task of understanding by themselves the divine will in all its implications. His reticence had no hidden motives. He was simply conscious of not being able to say anything for the moment, because he knew he had to go on sitting there for a long, long time in darkness and solitude, knew it would take time for the noise of the animals to be transformed into a background hum to fructify his thoughts, time for him to derive some inspiration from the bad smell of living bodies, and to reach the point of being able to say something to his family, himself, and God. For now he didn't even try. He confined himself to admonishing his family, almost crushed by the revelation, not to neglect the care of the animals. Then with a wave of his hand, he dismissed them all.

Let us dismiss them too, and leave them to begin a confinement full of hardship, suffering, and often danger. If after the patriarch's blunt statement, any doubt remained in their minds, it quickly vanished at the sound of the increasingly heavy rain beating on the walls of the ark; and the last shred of hope that maybe, in spite of it all, what the Lord had planned would not exactly happen vanished the moment the huge structure made its first lurching motion. The air vents, on the upper edge of the ark, opened upwards, but the overhanging eaves above them made it impossible to look out. The single large window was carefully shuttered and bolted, and had been placed at an inaccessible height, but even had it been accessible, it could unfortunately only be reached from that cubbyhole that the patriarch had reserved for himself, indefinitely it seemed, for his meditations. Opening the door was absolutely out of the question. Noah had told them that it was the Lord who had closed it behind them. But even if this statement was a little exaggerated, who would ever have tried to open the door when it was extremely probable that, given the heavy load of the ark, the stoop was now under water? They were forced to admit it: the Lord had locked them in for good.

So Noah and his family did not see the flood. Even if their curiosity, piqued by all that is terrible, sometimes tormented them, they ended by agreeing that it was better to see and know nothing. Their imaginations, in this case certainly quite poor compared to the reality, nevertheless offered them images that were terrible enough. While the ark still stood motionless on the meadow, under the torrential rain that was not to end for forty days, those inside often thought they could hear, above the pelting of the water and the deafening noise of the animals, their kinfolk, no longer unsuspecting, standing outside around the ark, rooted to the spot, in a dense throng, their begging and cursing and desperate pounding on the sides of the gigantic hulk already muffled by the excessive moisture. Inside, each of them wept and lamented at the thought of those beloved persons left outside, parents, brothers, relatives, and friends; and to a growing degree they suffered from survivors' guilt. Each, through his or her own torments, had now understood the patriarch and had rehabilitated him, bestowing in retrospect a remorseful veneration on his madness. But every sense of mourning, fear, suffering, evaluation, and re-evaluation paled before a single exultant and triumphant feeling: the joy of life saved. If hitherto, full of a sense of guilt, they had feared God, now they experienced a new aspect of their relations with Him: the gratitude of man, more miserable than a worm, for the mere existence of an omnipotent Lord.

So let us dismiss them, leaving them to spend their time in the floating zoo and resolve their sundry problems of a practical kind. And let us also leave the patriarch to meditate in peace in the dark and narrow cubbyhole, where after a certain time he was able to achieve those conditions in which even the chaotic noise of the animals and the stinking perspiration of many thousands of living bodies could fructify and stimulate his thoughts.

After the fruitful state of death lasting a year and ten days in his watery prison, Noah emerged from the ark a *new man*.

IV. The altar of the Covenant

When after the Lord's third message, the shortest of all and this time even reassuring, Noah finally left the ark and from the summit of the muddy slopes of Mount Ararat took a look at the desolate world, his chest did not swell in recognition of a job well done. We must absolutely discard the false image we have had since childhood of the hero of the flood. The disheartened old man who surveyed the earth drowned in mud and slime was by no means proud of the prospect that the life to come would be his handiwork, and did not triumphantly stretch his limbs at the thought that with his dry loins he would become the founding ancestor of the new humanity and, in a certain way, even of all the animals on earth. No, by no means: he now knew too much to enjoy any such feelings of satisfaction.

We have already alluded several times to the fact that in the fruitful state of death in his floating tomb, Noah had arrived at the knowledge of something. Later on we intend to spell out in detail what it was that he had arrived at the knowledge of, but it would not be proper to go ahead without at least saying a word or two about the peculiar nature of this knowledge.

In stating that the patriarch knew God's intentions with regard to the expulsion from Eden and the deluge, and that he understood them fairly well, we did not mean to suggest that he knew them in the same form and manner in which we explained them in the first chapter. We have had valuable help in our investigations from mythology and the comparative history of religions, as well as from certain insights of depth psychology, all of them recent achievements, thanks to which we have at our disposal an incomparably vaster perspective on his story than he, who lived within that story and indeed was himself his own story, could have had of it. At that primitive stage of conceptual reasoning, he did not even have the words to express a great part of his spiritual experience. But the incapacity to express himself was not merely due to the lack of adequate words. As we all know from our ordinary everyday experience, most of the contents of our knowledge do not lend themselves to being expressed in conceptual form, without thereby being any less real than those that easily clothe themselves in words, and without being doomed to remain unexpressed: whatever is of vital importance in our psyches demands a form of expression and finds a way to act on our existence. It would thus be unreasonable not to attribute to Noah a kind of knowledge whereby he understood and reflected on his own situation. As we will see, he even had his reasons for not uttering a word about what he knew. But the new contents of his consciousness were too essential not to be manifested in one way or another, and it is precisely the way in which they were expressed that allows us to reconstruct what he must have discovered during the fruitful state of death in the floating tomb.

If in what follows we express some of Noah's thoughts in the terms of our own language, no one should accuse us of inventing: we are simply translating some of the contents of our progenitor's mind into the concepts of our century. With the reader thus forewarned, we feel entitled to state without further ado that Noah, in his dark, cramped cubbyhole in the ark, came to recognize and understand the human situation resulting from the flood.

In the patriarch's meditations, the flood appeared less and less as a punitive campaign by God against the human race. If the Lord intended only to extirpate wickedness, the flood was nothing less than a fiasco. After all, wickedness, starting with Ham, the second of the three sons, was to be immediately reborn and to grow rapidly and exuberantly in the blessed branches of Shem and Japheth as well, right down to our own days. If instead God had only meant to sharpen the order of the curse, piling up new obstacles on humanity's path, this too would have been a gross error and an oversight scarcely worthy of divine greatness. Indeed, when the flood was over, Shem, Ham, Japheth, and their descendants continued on the interrupted path, and once certain preliminary difficulties were overcome, did not even notice any difference between antediluvian conditions and postdiluvian ones. Folk wisdom, which tells us that life—despite all historical evolution—always follows the same pattern, and that the history of human beings consists essentially in being born, suffering, and dying, expresses the eternal immutability of the human situation. This is how life, from Adam to our own day, goes on, and the flood, which did nothing to make it worse, could just as well not have happened. But folk wisdom, the common patrimony of Noah's children, does not take into account the crux of the matter, which Noah instead had realized! The crux was not at all that human life had become worse, but that the human position had taken on a totally and radically new aspect with respect to the world and the Creator. And this had been precisely God's intention: Noah, in his way, not only understood it, but was the first—and for a long time also the last—to do so; and he understood it in that phase of humanity's march called "the deluge," and in which he was *Man*.

From now on we must pay closer attention to this quality of Noah's, a much more universal and important quality than being the chief of a small tribe. For the tragedy of the flood took place *in* Noah, its meaning and importance became consciously concrete in *his* mind, determining the new human condition in *his* person. This fact needs to be emphasized so as not to see the flood as Noah's personal affair, even though it was so closely connected with his person. Besides, it should not be our concern to separate what was strictly personal in Noah from what was generally human. Everything involving Man, at that moment and for the future, became concrete in Noah, took place in him and by means of him, while Noah's personal affairs involved the whole human race. Humanity, at a very remote time and in a decisive phase of its march, comprehended itself in the figure of Noah: such is the nature of the mythological way of seeing. So we can simply narrate the vicissitudes of Noah instead of discoursing on a phase in the evolution of consciousness.

Of course, Noah himself—and this cannot be held against him—primarily considered the flood to be one of his most intensely private affairs, to the point where, although he was not entirely indifferent to the future fate of his sons, his concern for them was only secondary, incidental, and almost academic. When after a year and ten days of confinement in the floating prison, he finally emerged on the muddy slopes of Ararat, he believed he had only a single task, that of raising an altar for the occasion; his role, after all, already seemed over and done with, finished from the moment he had completed the construction of the ark and successfully embarked his family and the animals in it.

This was also, more or less, the opinion of his sons and the three daughters-in-law; not even his wife, that second Eve now rendered innocuous, thought she could count much on the taciturn old man for the future. And this has been public opinion down through the millennia to our own times. We should not, however, let ourselves be influenced by the mistaken beliefs of Noah, his family, and posterity, since they merely go to show that not only is the ordinary man incapable of judging at what point the mission of the chosen is concluded, but neither is the chosen himself, who having carried out the task assigned to him by God, thinks he has earned the right to retire. Let us admit that the salvation of the human and animal species was unquestionably an important act, sufficiently outstanding as to create the illusion that it was the one result of the great adventure, its meaning and the exclusive reason for it. We hasten to stress, however, that it is not only the exploits of the chosen that are important, since destiny also governs their thoughts and everything that happens to them, though independently of their conscious will.

The correctness of this thesis can be seen with particular clarity in Noah's destiny: unconsciously and unwillingly, and rather than at God's command, very nearly contrary to it, he persisted in his role, and while maintaining a passive attitude, continued to exert an influence on the fortunes of humanity no less than by his previous conscious action, to which we owe our survival. Indeed, if we like, we can assign a higher value to Noah's passive role than to his conscious activity, in which he was only a simple instrument of God, the apparent purpose of which did not go beyond the field of biology. His further passive attitude instead was already a personal "merit," an achievement of a spiritual order not demanded by God; it was the first human initiative *par excellence* in the course of history. Thus it was that Noah, who consciously was content to let humanity survive purely as a biological fact, in the second act of his role tried, not entirely consciously, or even unconsciously, to comprehend the position of the rescued human race and to let it survive spiritually as well.

For Noah, the ark, the black ship, was what in a distant future the bottom of the dried-up well would be for Joseph, or the belly of the whale for Jonah, or the stone tomb for Jesus Christ, a fruitful state of death from which it was a logical necessity to emerge reborn. The coincidences allow for no doubts about the similarity of these cases. The absolute seclusion from life and the world in a place hermetically sealed like a grave, and the subsequent resurrection to a completely new state, are, like the corresponding journey, characteristic attributes of symbolic death. But because of the particular nature of the relations between God and man at that moment, this symbolic death of Noah, the first in the history of humanity, in many respects differs, or even contrasts, with the later ones. Noah's extraordinary journey contained specific elements that are not to be found in other similar journeys. Indeed, while all the journeys to the regions of hell, whether mentioned in the Bible or in various mythologies and pious legends, meant an approach to the divine, the purpose of Noah's journey in the world of death was, in accordance with God's intentions, an estrangement from the divine. Every ultra-earthly journey started from the human to flow into the divine, while instead this earliest one led from divine possibilities to the utterly human form of existence. God, in fact, had decided from the beginning that a humanity of worse quality than the one swallowed up by the waves of the flood should emerge from the ark.

The first removal of man, the expulsion from Eden, had not fully achieved its purpose: the human being, at least as far as his possibilities were concerned, had still remained afterwards on an equal footing with God and nature, and the Lord had lost faith in horizontal displacements. So with the flood, by barring any other possible form of locomotion, He created the classical form of all symbolic death journeys, the one in a vertical direction. Of course, Noah's journey had necessarily unfolded in the vertical direction, but nevertheless, by its special destination, it distinguished itself from all such journeys to come. The Lord's intentions having been reversed with His favorite, the direction to follow in the vertical journey had to be reversed too. Indeed, as all known examples demonstrate, anyone wishing to lift himself to God must first descend into the kingdom of death to acquire the secret of the wholeness of being. Instead Noah's journey was an ascent, a continual rise to reach aerial space, the diametrical antithesis of the rich density of the kingdom of hell. That rarefied stratum was surely not the suitable sphere for arriving at a knowledge of certain divine things, but rather for forgetting them! The purpose was achieved. Noah, returning to his point of departure, found nothing of what he had left behind. The past, his and that of the human race, had completely disappeared from the face of the earth, without leaving any memory of itself. The spectacle presented by the desolate world finally made him understand, and with no possibility of doubt, that it was all over, everything that had or might have been, and now it was up to man, by his own strength, to create a new world from the water and mud puddles, a world completely different from the one before, and whose chief characteristic, compared to the previous one, would be precisely that it was an absolutely human world.

Never had the Lord interfered more ambitiously in the life of humanity, but having achieved His purpose, His feverish concern yielded to a joyous sense of triumph, followed by a contemptuous lack of interest in the annihilated adversary. He could hardly have cared less what Noah might think of the new situation: all that mattered to Him was that man should actually find himself in this situation. Thanks to this indolence on the Lord's part and Noah's meditations, the fruitful state of death resulted in a human resurrection *par excellence*, an altogether special resurrection, the exact opposite of all later ones, which were to lead from a lower human state to a rebirth in the divine. That of Noah, the earliest, was a rebirth from a hybrid titanic state to a peculiarly human existence: the reawakening of consciousness and criticism.

To Noah himself, it may have seemed that it was the enormous physical and mental efforts sustained during the building of the ark, or else the effects of his psychical and nervous collapse, that had made silence and solitude so welcome to him. In truth, all this was nothing but an excuse to devote himself to his meditations and continue his mission, albeit unconsciously and passively, a mission now required not by the Lord, but by his new human position. Having declared and demonstrated his complete lack of interest in everything that happened in the ark, he devoted himself to meditation, which seemed to him the only suitable and salutary thing to do. Man, who had forever lost not only the earthly Paradise but also the hope of returning to it, now had nothing to look forward to except to try to understand his own situation in the world, where he now lived dispossessed. In the fruitful state of death in his watery prison, Noah understood this perfectly, and emerging from the ark, was even more convinced that the flood had now separated man irrevocably and more inexorably than any cherubim from the world in which he might still have had divine aspirations, and that henceforth man could no longer immerse himself with ecstatic joy in the harmony of the cosmos, but found himself *facing* the universe, since he had been expelled from creation and become the Creator's plaything.

The results of his meditations, as they were transformed into the contents—though inexpressible in words—of his conscious mind, further increased the confusion and profound melancholy in his soul. The more he was able to reconstruct within himself the divine plan and understand his own role in it, the more it seemed to him that his simulated madness would end by overwhelming him, or that if he did not find a way out as his brain clouded over, he would destroy himself in the dark and miserable cubbyhole—so afflicted was he by his disappointment in the Lord, with whom he had walked for so long, and so gnawed by shame and humiliation for the way God had trapped him.

What a disappointment on the Lord's account! From whatever angle he looked at it, the flood seemed to him unforgivable: God should never have let things arrive at such a pass! Pondering the superhuman dimensions of divine omniscience and the deficiencies implicit in it, Noah came to the conclusion that one could not count on God, since even if He was good, just, and reasonable in a humanly inconceivable sense, to human reason He was unfortunately inconsistent, and not seldom bad and terrible besides. And if man was left so in the dark with respect to divine intentions, this meant he could not walk with God except by pure accident, and in truth was simply at the mercy of His will.

The covenant that the Lord had offered him in His first announcement, and which in the most natural way He had taken as having been accepted, now seemed to Noah more and more suspect and equivocal. Recalling the contracts that as a patriarch he had stipulated with neighboring tribes on the subject of trade, it seemed to him that these bilateral accords tried to serve the equal interests of both contracting parties. Instead the divine covenant, seen from the depths of the floating tomb, appeared to have a different character. At the moment it was offered, the covenant had appeared to be above all to his advantage, leading him to believe that his privileged situation was a great honor. But with the logical development of events, it had turned out all too soon that the privilege, however much of an honor it might be, was nevertheless and at the same time a disaster, for which he bore only the onus and which had driven him to the brink of madness. The covenant, indeed, served exclusively the purposes of the Lord.

In the course of his meditations, the second divine message often returned to his mind, repeating itself almost stubbornly and anxiously. On that occasion, God had spoken thus: "Come thou and all thy house into the ark; for thee have I seen righteous before me in this generation." Now remembering with obsessive frequency this first sentence of the message, with his tormented imagination he clearly made out a kind of malicious and humiliating cadence in the thunderous boom. The conviction that the Lord on that occasion had been pulling his leg once and for all, and that this would extend to his descendants as well, took on increasingly concrete form in his mind. His face blushed with shame and his tongue became dry with bitterness when he put the question to himself: Why should he have been the one chosen by the Lord to carry out this honorific and horrible task? What had made him worthy to survive the general destruction? But the question frequently came back to him in negative form as well: What had made him unworthy to perish along with the others? And in the depths of his tormented soul he felt that the question held up better in this form.

The answer was surely hidden in that word of the message whose true meaning he had so far never been able to understand: "The earth is filled with *violence* through them. . . ." What at the time had seemed a metaphor of the Lord's was revealed to him in the depths of the floating tomb as pregnant with meaning. The generation in which he alone had been found to be just was more than wicked in the sight of God: Cain's people, but also the descendants of Seth, all humanity thronging the surface of the earth, were truly violent, and violent by nature; indeed, all of them were still subject to the magical call of Eden and planning to return there by an iniquitous and violent deed, contrary to the divine will but by no means impossible, since the difficulties hindering it were only of a practical and not essential kind.

To destroy this potent and violent humanity was the task of the deluge, while his task, the task of Noah the just, was to give life to a humanity that would no longer be dangerous to God. This task had fallen to him because he was not of the race of the violent: he had always followed the order of the curse, walking with the Lord even when the latter was dozing. It was in the ark that the answer to the disturbing problem of "why now and not before?" was also revealed to him. Now he knew that in himself "something" had been opposed to the opprobrium of future existence, something that demanded the suicide of a race condemned to degeneration. In the ark he understood that for an instant it was he who had been the key to the divine plan. If he had paid attention to the secret voice and had not overcome his dogged sterility, would the Lord have been able to carry out the deluge? Would He not have been obliged to postpone its realization until He had found another Noah ready to procreate a degenerate race? And while the Lord was searching for another Noah, might not man, the violent generation, have perhaps been able to succeed in reconquering the lost Paradise? But he had met the Lord halfway and become dear to Him and was thus worthy of being singled out: which meant, on the other hand, having become unworthy of those sentenced to death, who excluded him from their ranks. The high and mighty, the aspirants to the fullness of being, the pretenders to divine existence had expelled him from their ranks, as a traitor to human prerogatives, the signatory to the compromise, the source of a base existence . . .

". . . for thee have I seen righteous before me in this generation." He heard the phrase with the malicious cadence re-echo from the walls with obsessive frequency, and wept, clawing his face damp with tears and burning with shame. So this was the covenant by which he had sold everything to the Lord for bare existence! And for the ambiguous gift with which the Lord honored him, the price would have to be paid by the human race, not to the seventh, but to the seven hundred and seventy-seventh generation, a heavier price than the one it had paid for original sin! Now he understood that with the covenant he had renounced once and for all the gift of the tree, and had resigned himself to man's no longer having divine goals, but being satisfied to the end of time with the artificial Paradise he himself had created! The covenant was nothing but a great compromise in which man, in exchange for mere existence, had renounced the meaning of existence, and had recognized his own nullity before the incommensurability of God. "To be righteous before the Lord means to become the Lord's servant!" he thought, weeping and beating his tormented head against the damp wall of the ark.

Fortunately Noah's journey in symbolic death exceeded the

conventional three days of his successors, and the period of a year and ten days allowed him to understand everything said above, confront the alternative of madness and suicide, delay the solution, and create for himself a way of behaving by which to pursue his life, which had now become burdensome and devoid of meaning, even after he emerged from the ark. He concealed his crushing despair under a mask, as he had done once before with his peculiar dismay, but this time the mask presented itself spontaneously: it was in keeping with the general expectations that from the silent immobility of the dark and miserable cubbyhole an old man would emerge, stately even in his prostration, who having brought a grandiose and horrendous task to its conclusion, would certainly no longer be good for anything. No one was expecting anything practical from him, not even an instructive word. Already in the ark, the youngsters were in agreement that they would treat him as a relic, an object of veneration, another Methuselah.

Under the mantle of stately taciturnity, Noah found a *modus vivendi* in the presence of his wife and children. With a resigned, almost compassionate smile, he dissimulated his despair, and did not even so much as hint at the knowledge he had gained during the fruitful state of death in the floating tomb. By his reticence he thus crowned the work of the deluge, because never had he walked so closely with the Lord as he did then, keeping what he knew about Him to himself.

But not even this time was Noah conscious of trying to walk with the Lord. Had he been able to follow his innermost impulses, he would not have built an altar with the wood of the now useless cages, but would have assembled his family and revealed to them all his knowledge and all the despair in his soul. But seeing with what *joie de vivre* his sons and their wives were wallowing in the mud and endless puddles, and the deep breaths they took to fill their thirsty lungs with ozone-rich air after the unspeakable stench of the ark, he understood all of a sudden that he could not utter a single word against the Lord that they would be able to accept. None of them would understand. The wisdom of his children had halted with the flood, and went no higher than the happiness of arid existence. Whereupon Noah stiffened in his stately taciturnity.

So at this point it is strikingly clear how Noah's role went through another important phase in its passivity, even after the deluge. It had been highly important to know all the things he had understood in the fruitful state of death in the floating tomb. But it was just as fatal for humanity that he should have kept his knowledge under wraps. Over the scarred memories of paradisiacal omniscience, new contents of awareness were placed, in layers, these too repressed and likewise destined to be scarred in the course of the millennia to come. At that moment, however, in their conspicuous fullness and vitality, they might have been able to change the fortunes of the human race. Would Shem, Ham, and Japheth have wished to live and multiply; would they have been able to continue their existence had they known the same thing, and in the same way, that Noah knew? In that case, a crazed humanity would have perhaps survived, to the greater glory of God. But instead, thanks to the reticence of Noah, who had walked with the Lord this time as well, his deeply buried knowledge was to reveal itself only by degrees, and much later, when the surface of the earth was already crowded with myriads of unhappy people, resigned to putting up with the artificial Paradise they themselves had created. The Lord nodded: Noah's reticence was equivalent to the deluge with respect to the survivors. Now, finally, the work of creation was complete!

Having surveyed the world drowned in mud and slime, and observed, partly with disgust, partly with pity, his children's *joie de vivre*, the patriarch, full of shame and bitterness, turned around and started walking toward the black hulk that lay like a lifeless corpse on the cliffs of Ararat, to collect from the now useless cages the wood needed to erect the altar of gratitude. In thus busying himself, he was simply going through patriarchal motions: his heart, devoid of gratitude and the fear of God, was absent. What he was doing, he was doing exclusively for the others, and this was the only thing he could do for them. Might the joy of living persist in their souls until they woke up! Might they remain unsuspecting until they understood the price of existence! Might they go ahead and prostrate themselves before the altar, thanking the Lord until they believed there was a reason for it! Might they go on intensely breathing the fresh air after the stench of the floating zoo, go on wallowing excitedly in the mud puddles until their joy of living changed by itself, and as it had to, into despair, until they realized they would never succeed in understanding the meaning of existence. That existence for which, day after day, grateful prayers would rise to heaven from the burnt offerings of millions of altars . . .

As we said, while he set out to assemble the altar of gratitude, gratitude and the fear of God were absent from his heart. Recently not only his ideas, but also his feelings with respect to the Lord, had undergone an abrupt change. And this could hardly be pleasing to the Lord. Thus Noah, who had had occasion to note that irascibility and an ensuing homicidal fury seemed by no means in conflict with the divine nature, could not categorically exclude the possibility that at any moment the Lord might strike him down with a thunderbolt. All the same, he did not take this possibility "seriously," either now while erecting the altar or before, when in the ark he had begun to think certain things about the Lord. For the most important of his ideas was that God could not be evaluated in human terms, and that if His enormous greatness consisted in this, it was just this fact that gave man a little respite. Man, though inevitably at the mercy of the Lord, could always count on the possibility that God would not constantly use His power. It was true, all things considered, that all manifestations and human acts seconded some divine plan, and yet God and man could follow apparently different and often diametrically opposed paths. Thus man, in his mental shortsightedness, could never know when his acts were pleasing to the Lord and when they qualified instead as iniquity in the sight of God. It might very well happen that while man was doing everything to act in accordance with God's wishes, the Latter, in His peculiar omniscience, took no notice of it; and it could likewise happen that in His singular onmiscience He was absent just at the time when man was committing some piece of wickedness. Even assuming that He noticed and took account of everything, it remained equally problematical whether He would react to everything and, if so, whether He would react in a way and according to criteria that human reason could foresee through the lenses of its own mental categories. In the final analysis, of course, one could put up no resistance to the divine will, but on the other hand things only rarely reached the final analysis, and moreover man could always count on the probability that the Lord's intentions were quite different from the ones he attributed to Him. This being the case, man, even in his state of bewildered enslavement, could breathe a little relatively free air.

Thus the patriarch did not deny that God was dangerous, he only asserted that there was no need to be afraid of Him, and that lightning did not come at the moment, in the form, and from the side that man expected, and might not even come at all. In short, Noah was convinced that for the moment he had no reason to be afraid of God; whatever he did and thought, he would not be struck by lightning!

He was so firm in this conviction that he overdid it, and for the first time after so long, felt a kind of relief. And as he busied himself, cloaked in a stately taciturnity, around the altar, and with a resigned, almost compassionate smile watched his sons and their young wives, in the excitement of the joy of living and the fresh air, bringing him the clean animals and birds (which had fortunately multiplied in the ark, thus helping in part to feed the unclean animals), the old patriarch thought that by this completely automatic action, with which privately he had nothing to do, he would finally be free of his role. Except for this burnt offering, the Lord could not ask anything more of him now, and if He had still had an announcement to make, it would concern his sons and not himself. All of a sudden he was surprised by the fact that his resigned and compassionate smile was directed not only at his sons, but also at the Lord: at the Lord, who having completed His work, found Himself in a state of emotion; He was handing down statements and pondering instructions for the humanity of the future, while he, Noah, now cared about nothing, was concerned with nothing, and found himself in the situation of being able to observe God's zeal with compassion.

When the pyre was finally burning, emitting an odor pleasant to the divine nostrils but nauseating to human ones, Noah made his wife, sons, and daughters-in-law kneel, and he knelt down himself. While the others, full of the fear of God and a sense of guilt, raised to Heaven their gratitude for their continued existence, Noah looked up with a wink and waited for the Lord's word. It was hardly possible that the Lord, anxious to enjoy His triumph and demonstrate His benevolence with abundant favors, would not want to speak! Had the right person been there, the patriarch would have been ready to make a wager with him that this time God would prove to be extremely benevolent and generous. But whatever He might say, communicate, or offer, nothing could surprise *him* any more. He already knew a lot, he already knew too much for the Lord to be able to surprise him again, and the time was past when, overwhelmed by astonishment and terror, he would fall to the ground as though struck by lightning: all this would henceforth be the role of his sons.

When finally, amid the usual roar and creak of the world's hinges, the well-known voice boomed over the peaks of Ararat, and the others, half swooning from the surprise, honor, and terror of it all, fell to the ground and duly prostrated themselves, Noah quickly overcame the unavoidable emotion of the first moments, and this time kept his ears cocked. Face down, in faultless immobility, he followed the words of the message with keen attention, and frequently shaking his head and frequently snickering, noted to himself that the declarations made by the Lord with pompous solemnity and as a sign of superabundant grace did not contain anything that surprised him; on the contrary, they confirmed to perfection the knowledge acquired in the fruitful state of death in the floating tomb. He could not suppress the impulse to comment instantly on the pathetic divine words.

Thanks to me—thought Noah, almost without remorse and if anything with a certain self-irony—thanks to me, the Lord is now able to be merciful toward the human race. My descendants will not threaten Eden, which has disappeared without a trace beneath the waves of the flood (meanwhile, with its tree, making even the fishes omniscient), my offspring will content themselves with the creation of an artificial Paradise in which dissatisfaction will be their destiny, and gratitude to the Lord will be their way out. This humanity procreated by me will be worthy of compassion and derision even in its highest aspirations, because while achieving everything that can be achieved by reason, its perfection will still be blind and deaf without the knowledge of the fullness of being, of which perhaps it will no longer even think. This humanity will perhaps be able to achieve omniscience, omnipresence, and omnipotence, achieve the immortality it has so far never tasted, achieve with a superhuman perfection all that is full of deficiencies and defects in the divine nature—and nevertheless the Lord will always be able to mock it. Thanks to me, who by desisting from my dogged sterility, procreated a harmless humanity for Him with my mad prolificness, the Lord can now afford to be merciful and generous, even good, reasonable, and just, maybe even by human standards. The Lord can now truly allow this soft, spineless, degenerate humanity to increase in number, multiply, and populate the surface of the earth, since this humanity will adore Him for millennia to come, and be grateful to Him for its own meaningless existence. But even if it rises up against Him, or learns to ignore Him, this humanity, thanks to me, will never again represent any threat to Him. May the human race go on and live, multiply, and increase in number—my offspring who, by emerging from my loins, made me unworthy to perish with the others, while had I not produced them, I would have jeopardized destruction itself! I, however, became worthy to survive, and the Lord, to document this fact, generously authorizes me from now on to feed on animal flesh. I will therefore eat the beasts whose salvation, it seems, I assured in part for this purpose too, I will eat them as a result of the honor of being raised above them by the Lord, at the very moment when I was degraded in my human dignity. Who knows why the Lord treats them so harshly? Of course, the dangerous shadow of human beings had compromised all living souls, so that now even the animals must share the sufferings of man. But did the Lord foresee this when He created them, long before creating man? In any case, with the change in the human position, the lot fell to them of fearing man, trembling before him, and serving him as food. You poor things, innocent companions of my vertical journey, from now on I will eat you . . .

With these and similar thoughts, profound and at the same time frivolous, with a mordant irony toward himself and a scornful piety toward the Lord, Noah, to whom no unpleasant surprise could now happen, listened to and commented on the divine announcement. He felt tempted to laugh in hearing the rhetorical promise that in the future there would be no more floods. He imagined the grateful relief of his sons. He alone was able to understand the intrinsic emptiness of this now facile promise. What need was there, after what had happened, for another deluge? He smiled at the idea that God knew it as well as he did; at the most, given the singularity of His omniscience, He didn't know that he knew it too. The visible sign of the covenant, the rainbow, which moreover they liked, was for him one more proof that he had well fathomed the substance of the divine prescience. For who had need of such a *memento*? Certainly not he, nor the human race. Had it been possible to speak to the Lord, he would have suggested that He invent still another sign, which, in case of necessity, could recall to Him the meaning of the rainbow . . .

Meanwhile the others were listening with due emotion and holy fear to the divine announcement, which kept dispensing boons, guarantees, and useful instructions for the life about to recommence. They still lay prostrate on the ground, as though struck down, and Noah, looking at them, thought how their souls were in disorder and their minds making enormous efforts to grasp the meaning of the bland divine words. And he thought too that although this message on Ararat had been clear and limpid despite its rhetorical pathos, none of his children or future generations would understand its horrible essence. For that, one needed the two previous messages, of which he had been the only auricular witness.

After his family had recovered and had duly admired the magnificent celestial phenomenon, which lasted for a while, the patriarch felt their questioning looks upon him. But he stared at them with an ill-concealed smile, then giving a slight shrug with one shoulder, said:

"You heard Him, so get going . . ."

And to the greater glory of God, a grateful humanity began once more to live on the earth.

V. The fated encounter

Having reached the last chapter of our tale, which also marks the end of the story of Noah, we pause for a moment, made hesitant by our suspicion that for some time a question has been forming on the lips of the dubious and skeptical. And indeed, the minute they get a chance to speak, they lash out at us. "Stop! Stop!" they cry. "Before you go a step further, put your hand on your heart and answer frankly: aren't you pretending to know a little too much about Noah? Don't you feel sorry, or doesn't it at least make you a little uneasy, to have dreamed up so much about your hero? All right, you've read something between the lines and exploited it, a little too freely in our opinion, but not without some justification. But where does it say that Noah had *understood* something in the ark? and where do you get the nerve to try to make us believe that you know *what* he understood? We've read the Bible too, and we've never found the slightest mention of any such argument in it . . ."

Although in some way we had foreseen that there would be questions prompted by skepticism and bad faith, they nevertheless give us a twinge of sadness. Deep down, in fact, we were convinced that our story, by faithfully following the Holy Scriptures, would turn out to be satisfactory both from the logical and the psychological standpoints, and thus would not need to be bolstered by further arguments and explanations. On the contrary, we confess that up to this point we had thought of ending this study with an effective and impressive last chord, and reducing the last chapter to a single sentence. This would have been the sentence:

"And then Noah planted a vineyard, drank wine, and got drunk . . ."

Our hope collapses, however, because of the suspicious questions mentioned above. The sentence that was supposed to figure as a solemn and effective last chord will instead have to undergo further treatment in order to justify the authenticity of the story and serve as our legitimate defense. Instead of reserving that sentence for the end, we must use it from now on as a bulwark against attacks by the dubious and skeptical. "Stop! Stop!" we cry too. "Be patient, ladies and gentlemen! Are you really so sure of having read the Bible, or at least of having read the story of Noah to the end? Or has it perhaps escaped your notice that Noah got drunk? For Heaven's sake, what if Noah's drunkenness were the key to the whole story? What if it's precisely from his drunkenness that one can deduce everything he came to know in the fruitful state of death in the floating tomb! Think about it a moment! If our ancestor hadn't come to know what he actually did come to know, would he have had sufficient reason to get drunk, the first man to do so, and in a paradigmatic way?

"The uneasy look on your faces eloquently demonstrates that although you may know about it, you haven't attributed much importance to the drunkenness of our number two progenitor. 'Indeed,' you retort, 'what difference does it make if someone gets drunk? If Noah accidentally got drunk, so what? What has it got to do with him? And finally, what has his getting drunk at the end got to do with the previous events in the story?' Be patient, ladies and gentlemen, be patient! Obviously, the last chapter will have to be written after all . . ."

Here is the passage to which we attribute considerable importance and which, in our opinion, is the natural conclusion to the great saga of the deluge: "And Noah began to be an husbandman, and he planted a vineyard: And he drank of the wine, and was drunken. . . ."

Before getting to the gist of the argument, we repeat our warning to skeptics and those who are in bad faith: they must get rid once and for all of the mistaken notion that one can find in the Bible or any other ancient text a single sentence, a single word, even a single accent that ought not to be taken into consideration. And this should come as no surprise, especially when, as here, the story is about a hero, the central character in an incomparable instance of divine intervention, a protagonist who by his mythological position actually exceeded the strict boundaries of individual personality to become *Man* in a decisive phase of humanity's march. As we have seen in Noah's case, events and facts in the lives of such eminent figures in our prehistory are important even when, though significant in themselves, they are not particularly stressed in the sacred texts. So what then should we say about facts on which a special emphasis is placed within the framework of a story laconically told, making them stand out as the writer intended them to? We can discard without hesitation certain facts in Noah's life—for example, that he surely sampled the meat of some of the animals he saved, or from time to time trimmed his fingernails. We would by no means do so, however, had the sacred text given special importance to the patriarch's meals or personal grooming habits. In that case, we could be sure that these facts had an enormous intrinsic importance, or were even of great significance for the history of the human race. But since the Bible stresses Noah's drunkenness, we are duty-bound to pay it the same serious attention that we would have bestowed on the two absurd cases previously cited merely as examples. For the very reason that it is explicitly recorded, we cannot skip over that memorable binge.

Therefore the inconsistent question—what difference does it make if someone gets drunk?—falls of its own accord. Without trying to drop the subject, we might modestly mention the fact that in every case of intoxication there is *something* worthy of attention. But the superficiality of the question has more to do with the *someone* than the something. Our interlocutors simply forget that the "someone" here is the ancestor of the human race and not some lovesick baker's boy seeking solace in wine because his sweetheart has snubbed him. It was Noah who got drunk, and this inseparable combination of subject and predicate seemed to the Bible worthy of special emphasis. Even granting that the patriarch's binge served as a pretext for events that are important from the standpoint of universal history—such as the separation of nations—the binge in itself still has an absolute and autonomous value. Noah drank and got drunk independently of being caught *in flagrante* and independently of the separation of nations, facts that were mere consequences of his binge. All of which is less important and less essential for Noah, and for us human beings, than the very fact that he drank and got drunk.

Now we can examine the other, much more superficial question: what does Noah's drunkenness have to do with him? This question, in its crude formulation, expresses a somewhat hostile attitude toward our conscientious methods, but all the same we see its point. What our interlocutors mean to say is that even though Noah got drunk once, we have no reason or right to imply that there's any connection between this fact and his great work. It has happened to many great and illustrious men to have imbibed a bit more than necessary at some time in the course of their lives, but such a circumstance does not in the least mar the grandeur of their deeds, and neither increases nor diminishes the importance of their position in history.

But here all the superficiality of this crudely conceived question becomes clear! It is indeed true that many illustrious personages of history, like millions and millions of persons in our own day, have got drunk and get drunk *incidentally*; but for this to happen, it was necessary that someone—in prehistory and outside of time—once get drunk *paradigmatically*! Therefore all those who refuse to see in Noah's drunkenness anything but an insignificant circumstance, as compared to the navigation of the flood and the salvation of the human race, are making a gross mistake, since this very binge was in itself one of the patriarch's great exploits, an organic consequence of his historical function. And our adversaries would be well advised to exercise prudence when, transcending the limits of Noah's person, one takes into consideration that he was Man himself at one stage of his march: it follows logically and with no impediments that at a certain moment in its evolution, the discovery of wine and the possibility of getting drunk became one of the human spirit's irrevocable demands.

According to the testimony of the Bible, if Noah was to get drunk, he had to discover not only the sweet mystery of the grape, but first of all invent viticulture, or rather, in one way or another, invent or at least reinvent agriculture itself. Thus the path leading to the binge could hardly have been a simple one in practice, but rather a long and wearisome one, on which Noah walked haltingly, and which up until the very moment of the binge did not guarantee the end or allow the final act of his imposing role to be seen. The fact remains, however, that it was precisely our founding ancestor who discovered wine, precisely he, and precisely wine, and precisely then.

Now we touch on one of the most enigmatic problems in the evolution of civilization, a problem that still lacks a satisfactory solution; at most there are ingenious and refined hypotheses that whet the imagination. How are the great achievements of the human spirit born? How is it possible that all of a sudden fire, bronze, or wine make their appearance in the life of humanity, unexpectedly, on a certain specific if unspecifiable day, while the day before no one had had any idea of them, and this although the preconditions for their discovery had already existed for a hundred thousand years? How is it possible that for hundreds and hundreds of thousands of years man had inadvertently lived with the simplest instruments, which lay within arm's reach and would have greatly facilitated his existence, and then virtually overnight had invented highly complicated ones, assembling them from disparate and heterogeneous elements that the reasoning mind would not dare to combine even today, and that moreover he had invented them simultaneously and at the most distant points of the terrestrial globe? How is it possible—going by the biblical chronology—that in the 1,600 years that had elasped since Adam, during the lives of nine long generations that tilled the soil by the sweat of their brows, no one, either among the God-fearing people of Seth, or in the race of Cain, begetter of giants, ever lighted by chance on wine, which might even have provided them with a little relief from their labors? How is it possible that some of the great inventions, though they would have been useful and proper from the beginning of human life, had to wait such a long time?

Far from being tempted to examine all the various explanations, we will only confront the simplistic thinking of the rationalists, whose ranks include our skeptical and dubious interlocutors, who are always so sure of themselves, at least when it comes to the things they leave out of the picture. Touchy as always when they stumble on the miraculous, they reply drily that it is of course not possible to invent everything simultaneously, and that for the birth of great discoveries you need a combination of favorable circumstances. It is, however, one of the rationalists' inveterate errors to be satisfied with little and fall into the trap of their own illusions. They do not realize that their arguments start from nothing and flow into nothing, and that the chain of their rationally linked thoughts is always suspended from the hooks of two question marks.

A tale charming in its simplicity will emerge if we imagine old Noah going in search of wine. We have every right to assume—and this should also be to the rationalists' liking—that after the great clarification that took place in the floating tomb, during which he came to understand his own betrayal, was driven to the brink of true madness, and was tempted to end his life, the taciturn old man continued to guard his personal independence in the presence of his family. Therefore he preferred to live, not in the patriarchal hovel, but close by in a separate tent of his own, partly so as to devote himself undisturbed to his own moral crises, and partly so as not to have to witness the energetic work of reconstruction by which his sons were determined to restore a life now devoid of meaning. It is also quite plausible that he left it all up to his sons, and preferred for his part to stroll about alone on the lush earth, which although teeming with new life, nevertheless produced mostly thorns and thistles, no differently from the way things stood after the expulsion from Eden. He went strolling about, partly for his mental equilibrium, partly out of boredom: and why would it not have been possible that on one of these occasions, on a hillside still covered with the slimy sediment of the flood, his attention was caught by some pulpy greenish-yellow and bluish-red berries growing wild among the shrubs in large, conspicuous bunches?

Driven more by boredom than curiosity, which had now sunk to a minimum before any of life's manifestations, the old man would have tasted one of those provocative berries and judged its flavor delicious. Conceding a point or two to the rationalists, let us even admit that after a while, having tasted the grapes several times and found them excellent, he had the idea of transplanting a few vines to the vicinity of his hut, so as not to have to go out each time he wanted some and poke around among thorns and thistles on the gentle slope of the distant hill. Then, by skipping over an uncertain period of time, we will arrive at a concomitant "favorable circumstance," the patriarch's toothless gums, which had difficulty crushing the skins, surely tougher in that primordial phase than grapes nowadays. This difficulty would have given him the idea of crushing a few bunches in a pail and consuming the berries in a liquid state. The juice of the vines was tasty, and the old fool, so as not to have to go to the trouble of squeezing bunches of grapes every day, and to ensure himself an abundant supply, would have spent a whole autumn afternoon filling the pail. Now after dinner and after supper, but also from time to time between meals and several times a day, he dipped his cup into the wholesome nectar, until after a certain number of days he realized that though he was sipping the same beverage, it had now become something else, better and more delicious, and in any case something that it was harder to stop drinking. At this point, he had *ipso facto* achieved drunkenness on the one hand, and invented winegrowing on the other.

This is the story of the discovery of wine *ad usum Delphini*, which ought to please the rationalists since it is full of such favorable circumstances as the aimless strolling, toothlessness, and folly, wholly excellent circumstances and, it would seem, indispensable preconditions for one of the most remarkable achievements of civilization, the production of wine. But unfortunately, much as we may feel impressed by such a happily successful reconstruction (which by its nature vividly recalls the story of Newton and the fallen apple), our curiosity is still unsatisfied: indeed, the question of why wine was discovered just at that particular moment in history still remains shrouded in mystery. On the other hand, we cannot rid ourselves of a slight sense of disgust: once having allowed the irrational factor of "favorable circumstances," why should we literally have to recognize them in toothlessness and folly?

There's the rub! During half a million years of humanity's existence almost everyone must have happened to see an apple fall off a tree, but nevertheless, until Isaac Newton, it never occurred to anyone to relate the incident to gravity: for this it took Isaac Newton. In the same way, we can ask whether there hadn't been any footloose strollers before Noah capable of discovering grapes among the thorns and thistles. Of course there were, just as there were people at whose feet apples fell. Indeed, there may even have been several people who tasted grapes. But it took more than just strolling about in boredom, or even seeing and tasting grapes, to lead to the cultivation of vineyards, not to mention the production of wine. Rationally inexplicable as it may be, the man who necessarily and inevitably transformed his own toothlessness and boredom into wine had to be Noah—Noah after the flood.

And there is another side to the problem. Noah, going for a stroll out of boredom and folly, surely saw other wild fruits among the thorns and thistles on the gentle slope of the hill. He would have found cherries, whose slightly bitter taste would have refreshed him and quenched his thirst; he would have found nice, red, fragrant strawberries, which would have aided his digestion. Certainly, in the course of his stroll he didn't stumble exclusively on delicacies, but also on ordinary, useful plants and seeds. Perhaps his eyes fell on beans, peas, and lentils, the last of which later attained considerable celebrity; cabbage and spinach may have been hidden among the many kinds of green leaves, foods surely suitable to expand the meager cuisine of his wife and daughters-in-law. But, oddly enough, the old patriarch felt completely indifferent and remained almost blind and deaf to the alimentary boons that spontaneously offered themselves among the thorns and thistles. He concentrated his whole attention, to the detriment of all else, on grapes.

No one can explain rationally why just these berries, yellowish-green and bluish-red in color, should have so fascinated him; not even he would have been able to give a reason, had his family asked him. They, however, were content to criticize him among themselves for this mania of his, which to them seemed downright useless for the consolidation of the new life. No, no one can explain, at least rationally, why from toothlessness and folly wine should have emerged instead of corn meal mush, just as no one can explain why out of the countless mysteries of nature, gravity was the one that claimed Newton's attention.

For centuries and centuries the beautiful princess slept, weeds grew on the streets of her city, and her couch became covered with cobwebs. A stranger, happening along, gazed astonished at the miracle, then bowing his head and muttering, continued on his way. Finally the prince arrived, bent over the lovely sleeper, and kissed her on the lips. And the princess awoke . . .

Might it have happened differently? Might others, and not the prince, have awakened the princess? Might he have married some other princess, and not the lovely sleeper? Oh, in vain did the pulpy and fragrant bunch of grapes smile sweetly at footloose strollers throughout the millennia: it was Noah who extracted wine from them. And in vain did the beauty of all the lush flora shamelessly offer itself: Noah chose grapes.

To rationalism, with its recourse to the favorable circumstances of toothlessness and folly, we truly prefer poetry, which unhesitatingly hints at fate fluttering over loving encounters of this kind. As we have already said, chance, for us, is a pretext for destiny, while the rationalists' chance is one of an infinite number of accidental combinations that might have worked out some other way, or even not at all. This trivial and empty interpretation of chance, which moreover explains nothing, is in conflict with our historical sense and our experience of how events of great importance operate. If it is necessary to hang the chain of our rational arguments from two question marks and resign ourselves to the irrational from start to finish, what need is there to substitute concepts devoid of meaning for the inconceivable, instead of frankly confessing our ignorance? If we are in no position to proceed, let us pause, moved by wonder, before the miracle, rather than letting ourselves be tempted by absurdities uttered in the name of reason.

Anyway we feel no obligation to linger in this rationalist blind alley, looking for first causes of the discovery of wine in Noah's strolling, or in favorable soil conditions in postdiluvial times, or needless to say, in the economic and social conditions of that unfledged humanity. To help us in our search, we already know a good deal about our ancestor and the circumstances of his life, and we have other knowledge that allows us to travel horizons much broader than those dreamt of by rationalism.

Within the framework of these considerations, such gratuitous hypotheses as the one by which Noah might not even have encountered the vine, fall by the wayside, along with the other by which he might perhaps have linked his name to some other great cultural achievement, the cultivation, say, of tea or coffee. Thanks to our knowledge, we can confidently assert that his was a fated encounter, like that of Tristan and Isolde, and his love was absolute and without hesitation: a *coup de foudre* that precluded the possibility of paying court to a coffee bean or a tea leaf, because when he stopped before the vine for the first time, his legs paralyzed, something in him, in the depths of his unconscious, definitely wanted wine and drunkenness and nothing else. Like Tristan and Isolde, who, in desiring each other, were in reality looking forward to the *Liebestod*.

In the fruitful state of death in the floating tomb, that is to say, the second act of his gigantic role, Noah had clarified his position before the world and the Lord, existence and posterity. The results of this clarification would seem to have been oppressive, even catastrophic, no less so than the flood itself. This despite the fact that he had reaped some advantage from his meditations in the dark, cramped cubbyhole of the ark, though not in a sense that can be appreciated by those with coarse minds. The incomparable benefit of such clarifications does not at all consist in leading us from a confused situation to happy, reassuring conclusions or immediate and practical solutions, but only in arranging the many evils in such a way that they lend themselves to being taken in at a single glance. And if in the lucidity of the clarification it turns out that everything goes badly in an unqualified and irreparable way, in this evil there is still a minimum of good: if nothing else, the fact that all this has come to light.

This minimum of good was all that was contained in the patriarch's great clarification: the only thing that had been revealed to him was that in the fatal compromise he had renounced the meaning of existence, in the name of all of future humanity as well. This revelation was in itself so horrible that it could not have been borne with a sane mind, and in general it was impossible to endure it and go on living unless one managed to go mad. If Noah nevertheless emerged from the ark alive and with a sane mind, this was due, even in the immense horror of his situation, to that tiny bit of good that consisted in the clarity of his views. The fact that he knew something, albeit the most terrible of things that man had ever been able to know, restored to him a crumb of his dignity. And it is in this crumb that human dignity still consists today.

In any case, the great clarification made it possible for him to clothe himself in stately taciturnity and gain time to meditate further on his insoluble dilemma. Indeed, he was still in a position to choose between madness and suicide. To persist in an existence emptied of meaning was no longer possible for him—for him less than any one else, because it was precisely to him that it had been revealed, for the first time, as devoid of meaning—or at least it was no longer possible to persist with a sane mind. All this was more than obvious, and it was only in order to make the choice that he needed to gain time.

This then is Noah's psychical diagram at the moment of his

emergence from the ark, that is to say, at that moment in humanity's march when Man realized that he had been wrenched from the harmony of the fullness of being, and stood there, endowed, to be sure, with conscious reasoning, but for the rest stripped and disinherited, thrown out of the All into the middle of a hostile world.

Noah, the patriarch, the navigator of the flood, knew everything that we have explained in our language and in terms familiar to our century, knew it exactly even though in another form, even while considering his own position as first of all (and understandably) a strictly personal matter. The divine messages, the ark, the covenant, and similar concepts served him as measuring units to evaluate the human position that presented itself to him as his own personal situation, or at most that of his sons. The crisis that had overwhelmed the powers of Man seemed to him primarily something exceeding his own worn-out powers. What he had had to face and endure since his early youth was really too much. The struggle sustained with his conscious will against his own dogged sterility, the moral depression that had resulted from it, the change of spiritual course following his furious fecundity, the Lord's sudden intrusion into his destiny, the frequent divine epiphanies that previous generations had been spared, the honorific and horrible task with which he had been entrusted, the desolate conflict between his duty to obey the divine commands and his own patriarchal and human feelings that had transformed his soul into a battlefield, then the ignoble dissimulation imposed on him by the situation, and finally the mental disequilibrium of which he never knew how far it was a game and at what point it became reality: all this had been more than enough to make him enter the ark as a human wreck. Then in the darkness of the miserable cubbyhole in the ark, revelations had followed one after another: disappointment as regards the Lord, the correct evaluation of his own privileged position, of the fatal and humiliating compromise—and of the covenant, more shameful than a slap in the face. He suffered from remorse in the presence of his children, now condemned through his fault to become slaves of the Lord, but he likewise avoided the gaze of God, who had made him His accomplice and could thereby mock him as well.

And nothing, at the moment of his emergence from the ark, nothing that could give him any relief! Looking ahead, he saw nothing but the endless desolate expanse of mud, slime, and puddles. And looking back, with the eyes of the soul, he likewise saw nothing but gigantic masses of water, water below, water above, the mass of shapeless and sluggish water before and behind him, and not Lamech's kindly, tired face or the living mummy of the indestructible Methuselah or the village with its busy life of the unsuspecting tribe. No, he no longer saw anything of the past, anything of what had been his life for six hundred years and had ensured it an organic unity; no, he did not find in his mind even a memory that could be spontaneously connected again to something truly existing, almost as though up until now he had lived in the void, in the immense tomb of the mass of water. No, there was no longer anything to which he could anchor himself, there was nothing to go on with: the great gray tomb had ejected him into the desolate void. No, it was impossible to go on living this way—or at least impossible to endure it with a sane mind!

Nevertheless Noah did not go mad, nor did he take his own life. He granted himself a reprieve so that he could retire into his tent and ponder what to do. Thanks to this momentary indecision, Noah arrived at the third act of his grandiose role, the discovery of wine. It was no big deal. The matter went more smoothly than you might think; in any case, it was much simpler than the childish fables of the rationalists. Noah truly found the vine with infallible certainty, just as a sick animal finds the beneficial medicinal herb.

This comparison is a great help to us in imagining how

Noah identified the drink, the surrogate and equivalent of death and madness, and at the same time it also provides an answer to some small related problems, like the miracle of *coups de foudre* and the chronological inalterability of great discoveries and inventions. Thanks to the progress of the sciences, and particularly to the inquiries of depth psychology, today we are now able to extend somewhat the limits imposed on us by those implacable question marks. Plato's teachings on pre-existing foreknowledge, discarded with a slight shrug by positivist-rationalist philosophy (constructed in its turn in the void), have today once again become plausible and would seem to be the only acceptable explanation for the origins of the most ancient and most genuine contents of our consciousness. The answer to the last *whys* of individual acts, thoughts, and aspirations lies hidden in the remoteness of the past and of the future, namely, in those dimensions of time with which individual existence has no contact. And to the *hows*, elusive for the logic of the reasoning intellect, an infallible answer is provided by instinct, guided by that *something* in us that *knows* the past and the future, and which, while it confounds us, also imposes itself on our conscious wisdom. That there is in us a sounder, vaster, and more ancient knowledge than our consciousness is no longer today a subject for debate.

Against the biblical background, this Platonic theory takes on flesh and blood, and we take pains not to detach our hero from that background. Certainly that "something" in Noah had already known wine since the beginning of his life, just as it had already known it in Adam and Eve from the moment they ate the fruit of the forbidden tree. Noah, Adam, the elephant, and the mosquito, they all knew wine, as they knew everything, having fed on the tree of omniscience. This omniscience was identical with the divine kind, and it was handed down from father to son. Indeed—and we must keep this important detail in mind—God had never hoped to be able to deprive man of omniscience, even though it was much less developed than that of any animal, due to the aforementioned undernourishment. The Lord could count only on this state of undernourishment and, first of all, on the intrinsic nature of omniscience itself: that is to say that although potentially perfect, it was nevertheless, in practice, full of defects and deficiencies. Omniscience, and the Lord knew it, was inalienable in man, it belonged to him essentially and substantially, and had it been possible to remove it from him without having to destroy man's very existence, there would have been no need for the flood. But if for some reason inherent in His plan, the Lord had to spare the life of the human race, He nevertheless, in a happy moment of His omniscience, remembered that along with omniscience, the divine deficiencies had also been transmitted to man, and they could not be remedied except by *anamnesis*, that is, by remembering at the right moment! So if it was not possible to suppress omniscience, it was quite possible to increase its deficiencies, simply by making it hard to remember things at the right moment. The expulsion from Eden, the punishment, and the proclamation of the order of the curse were to act as psychic traumas to bury omniscience and hinder its memory. This series of lightning actions was, however, only an obstacle to reawakening, not a guarantee against it. And that the danger of a human reawakening once loomed, despite all the precautionary measures, is demonstrated by the need for the flood.

It was, of course, necessary to liquidate humanity, human beings in their entirety, and first of all the accursed lineage of Cain, but no less the blessed one of Seth, because the fatal identity and ghostly assonance of certain names aroused the suspicion in the Lord's alarmed heart that the coincidences were more than phonetic, that they were also substantial, that the venerable Methuselah was a potential Methusael, and Lamech with his kindly, tired face a latent murderer. But beyond the quantitative liquidation of humanity, it was equally necessary to think of atrophying any divine impulses in the survivors, the future human race. The traumatic effect of the flood realized God's intention to perfection. Indeed, primordial knowledge has sunk even lower, and it has become even harder for Noah's descendants to remember it.

Nevertheless all of us possess the patrimony of omniscience, even if in an atrophied and moldy state, except that the paths leading to it are inaccessible or hopelessly arduous. The situation was, however, quite different for our forefather, a prediluvial or transition being.

Noah, or if you prefer, Man in the "Noah phase" of his march, was by comparison with us still close to the fullness of being. His primordial knowledge was covered only by a single traumatic layer, and what there was of omniscience in him was able to remember the essential with relative ease, indeed was capable of taking measures in his stead and against him, as had happened with his dogged sterility.

It should therefore come as no surprise if Noah, while taking a stroll, paid attention to grapes and fell in love with them. He stood there dumbfounded, struck by *amor fati*, and just as formerly his dogged sterility had been nothing but the recollection at the timely moment of the imminent deluge, so his fascinated interest in grapes was the timely memory of wine and drunkenness.

Thanks to the identical substance of omniscience in God and in living beings, it should not surprise us that the mechanism of its functioning in the two natures, divine and human, also reveals similarities. Just as the Lord, in His perfection, is apt to undergo long periods of somnolence, from which at the timely moment He suddenly awakens and remembers whatever is necessary, so man too, who lives in the darkness of his lucid intellect, sometimes remembers the lights of his underground primordial knowledge, with incomparably greater difficulty, of course, than the

Lord, but like Him, always when it is necessary. Necessity, most of the time not even informed by reason, seems to be what regulates our unconscious powers, awakening the most useful and most unexpected ones at the timely moment. It would seem that without the alarm bell of necessity, nothing can happen on the conscious surface. It made absolutely no difference that Noah's ancestors had seen, observed, admired, touched, tasted, and squeezed bunches of grapes: winegrowing and intoxication never emerged, because actually nothing in the world made it necessary for a human being to gulp down a glass of wine. And this would be the key to the chronological inalterability of all discoveries and inventions, and to every question of "why now and not before?" Necessity and fate make reality real, and to say "it cannot be otherwise" confers a tragic and solemn seriousness on even the most insignificant or foolish individual life that exists. Wine in Adam's or Enoch's cup would have been something fairly trivial, but it was an existential necessity in Noah's pail.

The comparison with a sick animal, while it indicates the common source of the subrational but instinctively unerring orientation, also reminds us of the actual similarity between Noah's condition and those of sick beasts. Indeed, when in the light of this comparison we examine the footloose old man's aimless loitering, we can immediately see that he was not looking for foodstuffs or aids to digestion among the thorns and thistles, but seeking his own salvation, the possibility of being able to continue his life. In vain did he eat his heart out over whether to choose madness or death: that "something" in him wanted life.

To go mad or kill oneself—these are the two possibilities left for the human being to escape the desolation and senselessness of existence. Many are those who avail themselves of one of these two possibilities, many who are able to choose. But much more numerous are those who find a way out between the two solutions. Many, following the example of our ancestor, take refuge in alcoholism. There is no need now to beat around the bush, and we can state with a clear conscience that when Noah went wandering over the gentle slopes of the hills, all he was doing, guided by the instinct of a sick animal, was going definitely in search of wine and nothing else. Because "something" in him knew that only wine would be able to cure him as infallibly as madness or death.

But within the boundaries of life . . .

Epilogue

Quod erat demonstrandum.
We will have fully achieved our purpose if we have succeeded in demonstrating that Noah's memorable binge is not an episode disorganically and disharmoniously tacked onto the story of that just and upright man, and if we have also been able to arouse admiration in our readers for the Bible's brilliant intuition in linking the deluge with the discovery of wine.

If nevertheless we do not immediately lay down our pen, it is because a portion of our readers, although they have followed us with benevolent attention, betray by their looks a painful embarrassment. We are quite familiar with such looks: they are the ones characteristic of unmusical persons on leaving a concert hall, or color-blind persons returning from an exhibition of paintings—they are the modestly offended looks of those who have understood everything except the essential. For us, who are able to enjoy Noah's gift and to appreciate its entire significance, it is perfectly natural that man, dispossessed of nature and thrown into nothingness, deprived of his divine aspirations, depressed by an inferiority complex, wavering between madness and suicide, without aims and without traditions, should set out resolutely in the direction of a tavern. But here the look of perplexity on some people's faces advises us to make a further effort to consolidate the results of our previous efforts, and to show a little respect for those who are color-blind and unmusical in relation to wine, and who cannot have even an inkling of what the state of drunkenness is like since they themselves have never tried it, while the experiences of others have always made a rather negative impression on them. We can see, rising up before our eyes, the proud and robust army of those who are sober on principle, the prohibitionists and teetotalers, as well as those who take only a modest quarter of a liter of wine with their meals and exclusively in the interests of a good digestion. Their perplexed looks betray the fact that they are still waiting for further clarification, and are exceedingly astonished that we take pride in being able to bring the heroic saga to a final conclusion, with our ancestor lying drunk in the middle of his tent, in a state of indecency that arouses no little indignation in his sons—indignation that the above-mentioned readers heartily share. And while we delude ourselves that we have arrived at the conclusion, the adepts of temperance and self-control urge us on to new efforts and demand that we justify our hero, or at least drag him out of the filth that he has spewed around himself. For, they say, it is impossible and contrary to reason and human dignity that a great man of saintly life and worthy of every honor, who has performed acts by no means insignificant and willingly or not walked with the Lord, should end up like this, at least in our story.

In their sincere respect for authority and in defense of the sober bourgois order, they themselves are the ones who anxiously rush to offer the proper excuses. All right, they say, all right, there's no question about it, given the testimony of the Holy Scriptures, our number two progenitor really did get drunk. These things happen, even in the best families. We don't believe, however, God forbid, that the patriarch became fond of wine! If he were alive today, he would be a teetotaler and a prohibitionist, precisely because he suffered such an outrage as a result of this execrable beverage. But how could he have avoided this awful experience? Wouldn't the same thing have happened to anyone in his situation? After all, there he was in the presence of a fragrant liquor with a delicious taste, and moreover above suspicion, since grape juice is absolutely harmless. Why shouldn't he have drunk it? How could he have foreseen the vile state that would be its result? Of course, such a disgrace happened to him only once, and as soon as he came to his senses, he threw away what was left, and from then on was careful to drink only the amount strictly necessary to digest the meat dishes allowed him by the covenant with the Lord.

The total incomprehension of a small portion of our readers makes us less despairing about this kind of comprehension from another portion, fortunately less numerous, namely, those who are sober on principle, respect authority at all costs, and take every word literally. Truly, we feel a pang in our heart thinking that our efforts have so far been in vain, and have therefore decided to make a further attempt, one that hitherto had seemed to us superfluous: to put Noah's drunkenness in a proper light.

No, you teetotalers and those of you who drink a quarter of a liter of wine to aid your digestion, we're sorry to have to tell you frankly, and beyond any possibility of error, that Noah did not resemble you in the least, and has no need of your excuses. We must repeat that his drunkenness was the result, not of his ignorance, but of a fated necessity, and that he did not get drunk by chance and only once, but in all probability many, many other times as well, as was more in keeping with his situation. But even assuming that he got drunk only once, his drunkenness was still atemporal, of universal validity, and took place in the name and on behalf of all humanity! And when he came to himself, he did not hasten to throw away the wine that was left in the pail, but offered it to Shem and Japheth as a consolation and remedy, and still more as a token of his own repentance and contrition, as a humble request for forgiveness for that existence that, thanks to him, had been saved and at the same time rendered meaningless for the whole human race!

We cannot leave to those who understand poorly or not at all even that minimum of satisfaction they might feel at putting Noah's drunkenness on the same level as the binges they themselves, alas, have experienced in their heedless youth, or have seen, heard of, or experienced thanks to others. One should not be allowed to forget that, from a certain standpoint, Noah's drunkenness was impersonal and suprapersonal and involved all humanity; it was the form logically necessary for the orientation of the human spirit in one phase of its evolution; it was a drunkenness universal in character and importance; it was the primordial drunkenness, of which every individual repetition in the course of history has been and is merely a poor copy. And we are sorry, but we cannot even permit anyone to make silly jokes about our progenitor in the form of excuses, to say, for instance, with benevolent malice: Oh, for heaven's sake, it's understandable, what harm was there in a little wine after all that water? Or: With all his worries, it was logical he should seek consolation! We reject such jokes, though they come closer to the truth, touching on at least one aspect of it, even if the less important or even negative one.

Besides, even if the beneficial effects of the juice of the grape did not go beyond the limits within which the joke is valid, no one would have the right to scorn them. But, we repeat, the soothing action of wine constitutes only one insignificant, indeed negative, side of its benefits, an aspect scarcely superior to its delicious flavor or digestive virtues. Every reality has its negative aspect, a surface of shadow, which is strictly related, however, to its entirety and makes its positive and luminous aspects stand out.

Nor does wine have anything to fear from other more serious and disgraceful accusations: that it is capable of lowering man to the level of beasts; that its effect is similar to that of death and madness; that it represents no solution since its truths collapse on contact with fresh air. Wine only protests the fact that from the pulpit of their sobriety stubborn prohibitionists and virtuous teetotalers hurl curses at it, and in their brashness forget that after all it was Noah, hero of the flood saga, who gave it to humanity, just as in other mythologies it was given by resplendent and divine figures. The nectar of ecstasy is a divine gift like the art of cultivating the earth, like music, like life itself. And the divine origin of wine is already in itself a guarantee that this drink also had a mission in life other than that of lowering us to the level of pigs and putting stupid, insipid words in our mouths.

In what does the divinity of wine consist? We, along with all those who dedicate a cult to the "divine" quality inherent in wine, cannot be persuaded that Noah, as a substitute for the lost Paradise and man's titanic aspirations, would have been content with the discovery of a sedative, which because of the marvelous similarity in its effects to death and madness, was capable of postponing burning problems and degrading man to the level of a beast, thus enabling him to endure his senseless existence by taking away even his reason, his last shred of dignity. Timely as it was, a gift that had only this to offer would not have been worthy of our ancestor, nor of the divinities of this or that mythology. Noah, when he paused spellbound before the vine, saw in it not only a sedative, but a medicine that could provide a remedy for his sickness and give him some hope of recovery.

Oddly enough, only in extreme cases do worshippers of the divinity of wine take to drink with the explicit purpose of getting completely drunk and achieving a state equivalent to death or madness—a state in which all problems are necessarily suspended.

At the most, this state occurs (and can even be expected) the morning after, in the form of nausea with all its disagreeable side effects. But the experience on which every drinker counts is the very adventure of drinking, with all its unexpected and unforeseen developments. The true drinker is well aware that drinking does not provide oblivion: what one would like to forget always remains present, and disappears, along with the other contents of consciousness, only when one is dead drunk. But this, as we said, is not the purpose but only one of the consequences of drinking.

Instead the miracle of wine lies precisely in the act of *remembering*. In that chamber, kept always at a constant temperature and illuminated by the same light, which is the surface of our consciousness, the divine epiphany of wine seems suddenly to open new windows, new aromas long banished enter and spread, and rays of light of the highest intensity penetrate the most remote corners, making things visible that had been completely forgotten. Up to now the nagging problem was enthroned as the protagonist at the center of the stage, but no sooner does the stage lighten and become filled with new colors and unsuspected life, than the protagonist's position also undergoes a change, all the more since new characters appear from the shadow of the wings; and all of a sudden it turns out that the true protagonist is to be sought among them, while the one previously in the foreground retires modestly backstage.

What advocates of sobriety scornfully call a retreat in the face of difficult problems, or an irresponsible flight from reality, is really nothing but a new statement of our problems: we courageously remember things that in our full mental lucidity we cannot and dare not re-evoke, and we place our everyday problems in the broader and deeper perspective of forgotten associations. The world that is thus unveiled before the drinker's eyes is much richer and much more real than the one reduced to the daily dimensions of reason.

Not even teetotalers and prohibitionists can deny that in the ecstasy of wine, or following it, many great events, great works, and great intuitions have been born in every field of civilization. The secret springs, to which only the golden shoot of the vine can lead us, remain forever closed to the sober part of humanity, while they reveal an immense richness of knowledge to the drinker. It is precisely this chaotic vertigo of richness that little by little makes one feel the "baleful" effects of wine. Stupefaction and confusion take possession of the mind that shortly before flew carefree: the light drives one crazy, the revelations kill. But the true drinker, priest of the divinity of wine, includes even these effects in anticipating his adventure. Recovering from his lethal sleep, he almost always finds a pearl in his clenched fist.

But penetration in depth is not the only feature of the ecstasy of wine: another is expansion, which provides the well-known sense of relief. The drinker, having reached a certain degree of intoxication, not only understands existence better, but expands and extends himself in existence; he himself becomes being. Life is revealed as something that exists for itself, and is sufficient unto itself, and in its new dimensions it is beyond the reach of any quarrel by our paltry reason. Knowledge and life never become identified, and the paradisiacal state of being is never so real as in the initial phase of ecstasy. It almost seems that the drinker has not drunk wine but tasted the fruit of the forbidden tree.

The passage from this state of fullness to that of death is not only not difficult, it is even desired and good, because necessary. The drunkard's collapse is the only tranquilizing form of "passing away," since it is inevitable—and death, by thus appearing as reasonably fated, loses its tragic quality. In this case, there can no longer be any room for discussion, as when non-drunkards die and reason can always rail against their unjust or premature end. The death of the drunkard is logical, it is the completion of fullness, it is his apotheosis. Fate is always good.

* * *

Since the purpose of this epilogue is essentially didactic, we hope we are not compromising the seriousness of our inquiries, carried out with the greatest compunction in the preceding chapters, if we now let ourselves be tempted by the wish to provide a description of our eminent ancestor's binge that can only be imperfectly documented. But our wish is not purely gratuitous; it also finds a place in the didactic nature of this epilogue. To make certain difficult things understood, examples are worth more than any disquisition. It is from this standpoint that the following poetic reconstruction should be seen, and we offer it to ourselves as well as a reward for the exemplary moderation we have shown in accepting the methods of the scholar instead of indulging the imagination of the writer.

When Noah, the primordial drunkard, took to drink for the first time (even if only once, but nevertheless paradigmatically and atemporally), he surely knew all the baleful effects of divine ecstasy, from the state of death in drunkenness to the morning-after headache, from the vomiting to the awful and shameful awakening, but he also knew its great benefits, and he never forgot them. It was the first time since the divine message, or even since the beginning of his whole centuries-long life, that he had felt his soul lighten up a little! Then, by a magic touch, he knew the happiness of paradisiacal existence! What until then, out of a fear of God and a sense of guilt, he had always tried to avoid now happened: his ideas wandered around Eden. And what so far had also displeased him in theory, namely, to have renounced great human possibilities by the compromise, he was now able to understand with his imagination, and to mourn it with real tears. Never, never again was he able to forget (nor repent of it) that when the repressed memories of Eden had begun dancing their celestial reel in his brain, he had all of a sudden felt suffocated in his squalid tent, and had to get wearily to his feet and drag himself to the threshold so as no longer to be isolated from the world by an artificial wall. Never had a sunset looked so beautiful to him.

With eager nostrils he breathed the warm air, full of unknown and stimulating odors, and stared with wide-open eyes, as though seeing them for the first time, at the darkened hills against the golden background of the sky and the shadows of the small garden, transparent and extended in the rays of the setting sun, while his enchanted ears absorbed the deep silence of the landscape, of which he had never before been aware. Everything seemed new, inexpressibly beautiful, and above all intoxicating. He had the feeling of being renewed himself, of being reborn in this miracle. He took a few steps forward, tottering a little at first like an old dotard, but then in his exuberant rapture, he rediscovered unsuspected energies in himself, his legs seemed to change, becoming suddenly elastic, and carried him forward with growing speed; soon he was already running, and a superhuman happiness took possession of his soul. His reinvigorated vitality forced him to run, to jump, to sing, and now behold, his decrepit legs launched him in flight across irrigation ditches, across cultivated beds of greenery and vines, and drew him irresistibly through fields and pastures, like a rejuvenated Silenus, while high-pitched melodies burst from his throat, hitherto condemned to gloomy taciturnity. He was no longer the master of his will: the harmony of the cosmos ran through his veins and governed his movements. Everything that until now had kept him isolated from this sense of well-being fell away from him, and at a certain moment even his garments seemed like intolerable encumbrances. Who was there to stop his enraptured hands from tearing off his clothes? For a moment it flashed into his mind that he was doing something crazy, but then he laughed at himself. The warm twilight breeze sent a delicious shiver through his stripped body, and in his huge desire to extend himself, he began to roll in the grass wet with dew, and even turned a somersault. He completely forgot himself: he recalled instead a handsome young man who ran naked to and fro on the island of happiness, in a solemn hour of universal apotheosis—he identified with the Adam of Paradise.

Then he felt like dying. Having crawled back to the tent, and as the beautiful world began slipping away before his dazed eyes, he thought the Lord wanted to strike him dead. But oddly enough, he felt neither fear nor repentance: it had been worth it!

Whether like a relapsed criminal, he tasted the clandestine pleasure many times, or tried it only once, but paradigmatically and atemporally, the patriarch, his brain hardened to reason, was able to know and appreciate all the positive and negative aspects of drunkenness. It was indeed a new and singular experience, and for the first time since the building of the ark he felt an urge to communicate.

So when he had recovered from his ecstasy, he went to the hut in search of his family. His sons were already outside tilling the fields, and only his wife and daughters-in-law were busying themselves in the kitchen. His unexpected appearance aroused neither pleasure nor surprise: instead he was welcomed with sullen looks that instantly robbed him of any wish to tell about the wonderful experience with which his heart was overflowing. Then he went outside, among his numerous grandchildren, and from their innocent childish lips he learned the cause of those sullen looks. The patriarch could feel his face flush, not with shame but with anger! These people dared to look at him askance? This race of ignorant slaves? At that moment, the contempt of drinkers for teetotalers was born, and in keeping with the nature of primary and atemporal events, it had its serious consequences.

Indeed, that very evening, Noah ordered his three sons to come to his tent. When they arrived, he was already seated at the table, on which the pail and three glasses were lined up. He was again very serious, even majestic, and bore no resemblance to the man who that morning had lain naked and soiled in his own filth. This clear contrast filled Ham with dark forebodings, but the other two also felt their knees trembling. The old man stared at them for several moments, partly satisfied by their terror and remorse, but while his fingers absentmindedly tapped his glass, a knotty vein throbbed on his temple, a visible sign of emotion. One could measure with the naked eye how his anger was swelling under the cloak of motionless taciturnity.

All of a sudden, pounding his fist on the table, he jumped up, and pointing his extended arm at Ham, cried: "Cursed be Canaan . . ."

He was surely a little high already, having taken a swig or two in preparation for the big scene, and the sons realized this, if for no other reason than the fact that instead of Ham, his degenerate offspring, the old man had cursed his grandson, an innocent child. But they found his other words equally confused and senseless, and it cost them much effort to understand that he was speaking of wine, a marvelous drink endowed with saving virtues and the depository of unexpected hopes; they could hardly make out that the patriarch was singing the praises of a divine liquor that Ham would never be able to taste because—and the curse consisted precisely in this—he would always have to live in darkness, he and his descendants, Mizraim and Canaan: their land might overflow with milk and honey, it might even produce magnificent grapes, but wine it would never produce, not so much as a pint!

Having vented his rage, he swayed a little, but did not sit down. His hands trembling, he dipped the three glasses into the pail. Then lifting one, he handed it to Shem, who had blanched, almost as though he had been the one struck by the curse. Then he lifted the second glass and offered it to Japheth, who had tears in his eyes. Finally he picked up the third glass, and going around the table with staggering but dignified steps, went up to Ham. Hypnotized like a rabbit before a boa constrictor, Ham watched him approach, and when his father stopped in front of him, barely a step away, the hand of the hypnotized son moved, automatically though uncertainly, to accept the third glass. At this gesture, the patriarch abruptly stepped back, and in his eyes the previous expression of rage gave way to a little flicker of malice never seen in him before. He fixed this withering gaze for a moment on his degenerate son, now more frightened than ever, then with a wink, like someone enjoying himself behind other people's backs, he turned to Shem and clinked his raised glass against his. "Blessed be the Lord God of Shem," he said quickly, while the flicker of malice did not leave his drunken eyes, adding, "and Canaan shall be his servant." With a light, graceful movement, he turned again to Ham, and raising the glass, almost as though drinking to his health, he drained it to the bottom. And all this was repeated in exactly the same manner, with impressive deliberation and a light and graceful malevolence, for the blessing of Japheth.

Shaking off finally the dutiful solemnity of great moments, he threw Ham out of the tent with a few now spontaneous bursts of invective. Then making himself comfortable on the wooden seat covered with goat skins, he bade the two sons he had blessed to sit before him on the bare earth, and began to speak:

"Yes, boys, bless the Lord and follow His commands, because now there's no other way," he said, with a touch of melancholy in his voice, while the malice sparkled one last time in his eyes, "and let yourselves be guided in your path and in His glory by your reason. But—" and at this point he raised his voice and hand—"but if the time comes in your life, as it must necessarily come for every son of man, when you realize in astonishment that the order around you is unreasonable and in you reason is disordered, so that you find yourselves caught in a crushing despair that makes life and the world seem desolate and meaningless and offers no way out, then do not hesitate to approach the pail and pour yourselves some of its contents. Because, you see, a miracle will happen. Suddenly you'll see that existence is not meaningless after all, but is stupendously beautiful and good, and the purpose of living is nothing but this fullness of being itself. Do not be disgusted if you do crazy things and fall into a state similar to death; and don't take it badly if some ill-mannered urchin makes fun of you. Don't worry when the ecstasy fades and what you have known seems no more than a dream, for you will come back as new or renewed men, enriched by unexpected knowledge, like someone who has traveled the circles of the beyond. But knowledge is not hidden in ecstasy and dream, but rather in yourselves, buried under an impenetrable crust of layers of oblivion that keep growing in number and weight, under a crust that resists any solvent invented by the human mind, resists the sharpest and most lucid intellect and the strongest and most decisive will, a crust harder than stone, but which becomes transparent and dissolves under the chemical action of wine. Take care not to drive away, like memories of a foolish dream, what you have seen and felt in your drunkenness. On the contrary, keep it in mind and use it to fertilize the barren field of your reason. If then . . . if then . . ."

He paused, and a threatening spark darted in his aged eyes. Shem and Japheth listened to him, their heads spinning, and the look on their faces expressed the confusion of men who would need several thousand years to grasp the meaning of these luminous words. Meanwhile, outside in the darkness, at the entrance to the tent, a number of grandchildren were crowding together and giggling among themselves. After pausing a while in search of the right words, the patriarch went on:

"If man should once succeed in remembering everything that the 'something' in him knows very well, then . . . then life would become beautiful again, as beautiful as though it were spent in endless intoxication . . . Then everything would be as beautiful as in Paradise . . ."

Fondly he caressed the glass, raised it to his mouth, and took a sip. Then a bitter smile appeared on his lips.

"But watch out!" he added wearily. "As soon as man is capable of living in the intoxication of existence without the help of wine, the Lord will no longer remember the meaning of the rainbow. Watch out, boys . . ."

"Grandpa's drunk again," one of the grandchildren announced at this point in the kitchen.

At the same moment in heaven, the Lord, listening to Noah, went pale. Here again was something that He, in His singular omniscience, had not foreseen!